TIME'S CURSE

HIGHLAND TIME-TRAVEL PARANORMAL ROMANCE

ANN GIMPEL

CONTENTS

TIME'S CURSE

HIGHLAND TIME-TRAVEL PARANORMAL
ROMANCE

By
Ann Gimpel
Elemental Witch Series

Copyright Page

Beware of witches, especially ones who pretend not to be...

Born a Roskelly witch, Liliana's spent most of her life running from who she is. Wielding dark power is dangerous, seductive. Mostly, she passes as human—until a clumsy spell lands her in 1890s Glasgow, and her web of fabrications collapses. Blackest of Black Magic workers, her Roskelly kinswomen are on the move. Risen from their crypts, they've set their sights on anyone standing in their way.

Sean makes certain Druid wealth remains invisible. Consumed by the seedy world of offshore havens, he's caught unaware and shanghaied backward in time. Furious at being targeted, he vows any witch who crosses his path will die a fiery death. He may have pissed off the Roskellys, but he'll make damn good and sure they rue the day they bullied him.

He tracks Liliana, intent on using his power to flay skin from bone, but something about her brings him up short. She may be a Roskelly, but the taint of wicked power isn't obvious. Beyond that, she's so alluring, she steals his wits. No longer hellbent on her destruction, he shrouds himself in invisibility determined to sort things out.

CHAPTER 1

*L*iliana Curtis sank to a crouch still clutching her cell phone in a death grip. She'd given ground. A whole lot, truth be told, but what choice was there? At least Katerina, her well-loved daughter, was safe for the moment.

Safe and about to be wed to a Druid high priest. One who was no doubt teaching her magic as fast as she could absorb it. Liliana blew out a harsh breath. Her strategy had been to conceal Kat's witch heritage, bury it so deep her daughter grew up thinking magic was a crock.

That approach had worked—until Kat's recent trip to Scotland. Liliana had done her level best to stuff the cat back into the bag, but it was too late. Kat was thirty-five, a respected anthropologist, and she'd been dragged backward in time. Twice. Of course, she'd reject her mother's staunch instructions to return to California immediately.

Liliana hissed in frustration, feeling witch power rise within her. She may have legally changed her name from Roskelly to Curtis, but it hadn't done shit to alter the dark magic that was her birthright.

Born a Roskelly witch, she'd shunned the wicked power licking at her heels. Her own mother—Gloria—had done the same, which made things easier. At least she'd had an ally. Most of the time. When she'd become pregnant, her mother had told her in no uncertain terms it was a mistake to perpetuate their line. She hated to admit it, but her mother had been right. Not much she could do about it, though.

Defiance only went so far. It was long past time to figure out what to do now that her daughter had discovered the truth.

Liliana splayed her hands on the hardwood floor, so she wouldn't fall over. She didn't often allow herself to think about Katerina's father. He'd been the love of her life, but he hadn't had a shred of magic. Not a lick. Not a flicker. Loving her had sealed his fate. If she'd had the strength to walk away, even after they'd conceived a child, he'd still be alive.

She winced and blinked furiously, determined not to cry. Old history was just that. Old. Warren's death didn't hurt any less, though, for being long buried in the past. She rolled her shoulders and rocked back on her heels.

Rhea Roskelly was her ancestor and one of the most powerful Black Witches ever born. Steeped in wickedness, she'd lived almost three hundred years. The old witch had been thrilled by Katerina's birth, mostly because it gave her another chance to perpetuate the Roskelly bloodline.

Liliana clenched her teeth until they ached. Rotten and self-serving to the core, Rhea had shown up in the hospital, and then suggested moving in to help care for her great-great-granddaughter.

Warren, bless his innocent soul, had fallen in love with the idea.

Of course, Rhea had sprinkled gobs of charm around, liberally laced with compulsion spells to manipulate Warren into agreeing. Liliana felt stuck. Wiped out from giving birth, and focused on her newborn, she'd let things ride for a while, figuring the harm would be minimal. Turned out "a while" had been far too long. Warren and Rhea became thick as thieves—because she was feeding from his energy.

Black witches did that—strengthened themselves on humans—but they far preferred misery to joy. First, Warren's father died under mysterious circumstances. The man just keeled over at his desk one day. A few weeks later, his mother was run down in the street by a drunk, and Liliana saw the writing on the wall. Kat was only three months old then, but magic was already stirring within her, no doubt a product of Rhea's meddling. The child could look at the carousel suspended above her crib and make it dance and turn. Delighted, she'd clap her chubby hands together and do it again.

Liliana did her damnedest to oust Rhea, but the old woman's magic far exceeded hers. Worse, Warren had turned from a sweet, kind man to an embittered, taciturn shell from witch poisoning. She'd never seen it firsthand, but it was easy to recognize, and there was no going back.

Frantic, she'd tried to craft an antidote, but Rhea had her claws sunk in too deep.

Liliana had walked in on Rhea and him one day. Warren looked like a corpse, eyes shut, head thrown back as inhuman guttural growls issued from his throat. Rhea rode him with abandon, straddling his skin-and-bone hips. Neither of them noticed her, so she sent her own magic spinning in an arc.

Testing. Hoping.

Hope fled fast.

Warren's soul was gone, replaced by a seething dark place. Liliana had blinked back furious tears and sheathed her power. No saving him, and she wasn't strong enough to take on her ancient kinswoman.

Enraged, helpless, she'd backed out of the room, snatched up her baby, and made a run for her mother's house.

Gloria lived six hours away in Nevada. Teleporting with a baby held risks, so she'd driven. By the time they'd gathered forces with a few other White Witches and returned to Liliana's, Rhea was gone and Warren's body putrefying in the same upstairs bedroom where she'd last seen him.

There'd been an inquest, but magic smoothed everything over, and Warren joined his parents in the local cemetery.

Liliana pushed upright. Her eyes stung, but crying was a waste of time. She'd always carried guilt for Warren, but the hard truth was she was also responsible for his parents' untimely deaths. If she'd been more on top of things...

"Stop it." Doubling up a fist, she punched the back of a sofa. Her hand smarted, but she deserved to hurt. Magic was an enormous responsibility, and she'd been the witch on duty. The one who should have intervened.

After Warren's death, she and Gloria had turned their lives into a campaign to keep Katerina safe. Despite their diligence, Rhea had almost broken through, nearly completed the ceremony that would have sealed Kat's fate and bound her by blood to Black

Magic. It was the final straw. Gloria, who like all White Witches, was sworn never to use her magic to influence outcomes, did what she needed to ensure Rhea was remanded to a mental hospital. The old witch ended up in a locked ward where she sat out her remaining days in shackles to mute her power—and make certain she didn't teleport out of there.

As far as Liliana knew, Rhea was dead. The hospital had given them the news shortly after Kat's tenth birthday. The little girl had been devastated. She'd loved her great-great grannie, but Rhea had also planted magical markers, enchantments to ensure Kat would long for the impossible—a life with Rhea by her side.

Her cell jangled about the same time as the pager clipped to her belt buzzed. Liliana gritted her teeth. Had to be the hospital. She snatched up the phone, clicked the display, and said, "Dr. Curtis."

"Sorry to disturb you on your day off—"

"Never mind that. What do you need?"

"Mrs. Johnson is dying. She's asking for you, and she won't last until you're due back in tomorrow night."

"I'll be there in half an hour." She rang off before the clerk could thank her—or deliver any more news that would require her presence in the hospice wing of San Francisco General Hospital.

Liliana loped for the stairs, intent on changing into

scrubs, her normal hospital garb. She lived in a remodeled Victorian in the city's Marina District. It was the same house she'd been born in, and she loved it fiercely. It was alive in a way newer structures could only dream of being. She'd moved back there after Warren's death and never left.

One of the upstairs bedrooms had been converted into a combination sewing room/changing area to keep her potentially contaminated hospital garb away from her primary closet. Neatness wasn't her forte, but she tried hard, mostly because she hated having to rewash something that had sat in an untidy pile on the floor.

Hanging garments as she removed them, Liliana slid into a dark blue scrub top and matching pants. She'd promised her daughter a long-overdue explanation of why she'd kept the Roskelly side of things hush-hush. Part of that talk would have to include the truth about Warren. Kat thought her father had died on a medical mission to sub-Saharan Africa.

Liliana hadn't ever had the heart—or the stomach— to fess up about what really happened. Besides, explanations hadn't been possible while Kat didn't believe magic existed.

She gave herself a quick once over in an antique oak full-length standing mirror before dragging her hospital ID around her neck. Green eyes stared back at her. Set in a strong-boned face with a square jaw and high cheekbones, her almond-shaped eyes held a hint of Asian blood. Jet-black hair would have fallen past her waist, but it was tucked into its usual bun, a long queue she wound low at the base of her neck.

Satisfied she'd pass muster—because she did not want anyone looking too closely at her—she snatched up her medical bag and her computer carrier. Realizing she didn't have shoes on, she put everything down to rustle in a corner for black leather loafers.

Finally ready, she retraced her steps. The large, empty house echoed around her. Filled with antiques —except she'd bought them new—the furnishings, paintings, and knickknacks matched the home's nineteenth century construction.

Liliana drove automatically. She liked Christine Johnson, a woman in her late nineties whose body had simply worn out. She'd been sunk in a delirium this past week, but everyone had a few hours of lucidity before they died.

Almost everyone, anyway. Too much medical intervention, which translated to too many drugs, could rob the dying of their last chance to tell their loved ones farewell.

During that time—the lucid spell—Liliana prepped their soul, shepherding it toward the proper passageway. After losing Warren, she'd devoted her professional life to ensuring no souls ended up shanghaied by darkness. She'd been an emergency room doc before her life turned upside down. It was only after Rhea sucked Warren dry of anything remotely resembling humanity that Liliana had secured a fellowship in end-of-life care.

She'd been doing hospice work ever since. Enjoyed it because she eased people's suffering as they exchanged one plane of existence for what came next. Being able to see spirits—and demons and ghosts—helped immensely.

She turned into the multistory hospital parking garage and headed for the physician parking area. Good thing she was here because she needed to talk with administration. Not that she couldn't have finessed that from anywhere, but it was easier from the hospital. She never took any time off. What would she do with it? She'd done all the traveling she wanted to, and she got bored and restless staying home.

After pulling into a likely parking slot, she gathered her bags and stepped out of her Tesla. The all-electric car had been a bit of a pain in the rump because small things kept breaking, but the company had fixed every last one of them. As she hurried inside, she considered how much time off to request.

She needed to locate her mother, so she could fill her in on everything that had transpired with Kat. One smallish problem was Gloria was supposedly dead.

Except she wasn't. She'd retreated to the later part of the 1800s, one of her favorite time periods, and was living in Glasgow. At least that's where Liliana thought she was.

Not much communication across time. Witch magic wasn't strong enough to accommodate it. She made her way to her small office located next to the hospice ward and hoped to hell her magic would be up to the task of splitting the veils of time. She hadn't done much more than ferry souls to the afterlife for the last twenty years.

The message light flashed on her phone. She ignored it and dialed the extension for HR. No reason to settle into the comfortable desk chair. She wouldn't be in her office long enough to bother.

"Good morning," a cheerful receptionist's voice chirped.

"You're chipper for it being this early," Liliana shot back. "It's Dr. Curtis. I've had a bit of a family emergency crop up. I'm working now, but when I leave, I'll be gone for the next two to three weeks."

Keys clicked from the other end, and Liliana cursed her hypersensitive hearing. All her senses were far sharper than any human's, thanks to her witch blood.

"My goodness, Doctor. It doesn't appear you've ever taken any of your vacation time."

Liliana rolled her eyes. "No. I haven't. Look, I'm not asking permission. I'm telling you I won't be here."

"It's fine, Doc. The staff from your ward will keep you apprised via phone."

She screwed her mouth into a moue. "Um, that might not be possible. I'll be out of cell range."

"Wow! Where are you going?" The clerk hurriedly added, "Sorry. It's none of my business. I'll be sure to note you won't be available by phone." A pause. "What about email?"

"No." She bit back a growl. "I've earned my off time. The other two hospice docs can cover the unit while I'm gone."

A rapid intake of breath was followed by, "Yes, Doctor. Of course, Doctor. Was there anything else you needed from HR?"

Liliana considered an apology for being surly but decided against it. She needed to sit with Christine. It was why she was here. She could have called hospital administration from anywhere.

"Nope. I'll check in as I can."

"Very good. Have a lovely rest of your day." The clerk disconnected.

Liliana dropped the receiver into its cradle and glanced around the overflowing shelves covering three walls of her office. The fourth housed a window, or it, too, would probably be filled with medical texts, journals, and other trappings of her trade.

She loved medicine, had been a healer in one iteration or another for the last hundred plus years. Her age was one reason she'd been so delighted—and surprised—to conceive Katerina. And why terminating the pregnancy like her mother urged was out of the question.

Modern science had changed medical practice, and not in especially good ways. Some doctors hardly even looked at their patients, let alone talked with them for very long. Computer programs had reduced treatment to algorithms. If X, then Y. If Y, then Z. It was only the true outlier diseases that received more than cursory attention. Most of her colleagues were more invested in avoiding lawsuits than anything else. It translated into reams of unnecessary tests that did nothing but drive insurance rates up—and insurance reimbursements down.

"Not going to fix that problem. Not today and probably not ever," she muttered as she trotted out of her office. She'd stop and get the latest on Christine from the head nurse.

And then she'd worry about her rusty magic and how the hell she'd manage something as complicated as a time-travel casting.

Christine's passing had been one of the more numinous ones. Liliana had sat with the woman for a while after death claimed her. Birth and death were two of the mysteries. How life begins—and how it ends. Because Christine was open to it, she'd linked with her mind, not bothering to be subtle about things. The woman had relaxed into Liliana's reassurances all would be well and embraced the brilliant, blinding light.

Her task as guardian of newly departed souls complete, she'd left the hospital, her mind overfull with all the things that needed to happen before she could leave.

A quick glance at a wall clock told her it was pushing six at night. She'd been home for a couple of hours. It had taken that long to locate everything she needed for her casting. Including a grimoire moldering in a far corner of her library.

Said tome was spread open on the floor in front of her, offering its wisdom. Getting it to talk with her had been her first task. Magical books weren't indexed and they either took pity on you and showed you what you needed...

Or not.

Maybe because she'd neglected this book so badly, it had taken its sweet time offering answers.

She assessed her hastily assembled outfit with a critical eye. In an attempt to not stick out like a sore thumb, she'd located a long, black skirt and lace-up black boots with flat soles—in case she had to run. A blue long-sleeved tunic was topped with a light jacket and a black woolen cape that fell to knee level. No zippers. No metal fasteners. She'd tucked a small assortment of medical paraphernalia into her many pockets. She knew better than to bring electronics with her. For one thing, there wasn't much point. They wouldn't work, and they'd be a dead giveaway she wasn't who she was trying to pass herself off as.

She'd be damned if anyone would get close enough to frisk her, but women had zero rights where she was heading. She might not have much choice about who laid their grubby, grimy hands on her.

Liliana checked the progression of her spell, noting it was about halfway to maximum velocity. She'd taken her time inscribing a pentagram on the basement floor but carefully drawing all the elements correctly hadn't been sufficient. Another witch, one who'd actually practiced magic actively over the past few years, could have simply barked the words and been gone, but she'd tried that. The light illuminating the pentagram had sputtered and died, almost as if it was laughing at her paltry efforts.

So she'd backtracked. Apparently, she lacked the skill for magical shortcuts.

Pages rustled, threatening to conceal the needed spell.

Liliana leapt forward and slapped a hand across the open book. "Oh no you don't," she adjured and refocused her attention until one hundred ten percent was on her casting. Not on Christine Johnson. Not on running checklists through her head to satisfy herself she hadn't forgotten anything.

The pentagram brightened.

Liliana blew out a frustrated breath. It would be so much easier if Gloria would materialize. Surely, she knew what was going on, that Rhea had dragged Katerina back to the 1700s.

A bleak thought surfaced. Maybe her mother had been abducted by her Roskelly kinswomen. Rhea was still very much alive at the tail end of the nineteenth century, and Scotland was her preferred playground. The more Liliana thought about things, the surer she was her own mother might be in deep trouble. Gloria's magic was strong. Twice as robust as Liliana's had ever been.

Rhea hadn't taken it well when her own daughter spurned her.

Liliana's fledgling spell flickered, started to fade. She growled annoyance. Done babying it, she jumped into the center of the pentagram, chanting like a madwoman. Her Gaelic was as rusty as her magic, so she butchered a few of the words, but the spell developed a life of its own.

Finally.

She'd cast enough complicated spells as a much younger witch to recognize the energy pattern that meant the casting had passed a point of no return. If she'd done things right, she'd be sucked into darkness and spit out in 1895 Glasgow. She hadn't wanted to show up too early and have to try again, so she'd aimed for the middle of the 1890s.

The air around her turned incandescent and thickened with the distinctive feel of witch magic mingled with the smells of her own power. Marigolds, vanilla, and sunbaked clay. Tingling started in her feet and worked its way up her body, sweeping her along with it. She loved the feel of casting power, adored the sense of invincibility and strength.

The walls of her basement fell away, leaving her floating in a dark void. She kept every fiber of her being homed in on her goal. It wouldn't do to fall off the grid as she dreamed of being Superwoman. She did not want to get stuck in the dark place between worlds and time periods.

Liliana set her jaw in a determined line, teeth jammed against each other. She'd do her best to cushion her sudden appearance with magic so as not to alarm anyone who might be privy to her entrance.

And then she'd use a tracking spell to locate her mother. It was blood linked, which meant it would also pinpoint every Roskelly witch in close proximity. Not ideal, but it couldn't be helped. The best she could hope for was that she'd locate Gloria before the Black Witch Roskellys noticed her presence.

I'm being ridiculous. What the hell could they do to me?

Answers rushed in from all sides of the blackness surrounding her. Each one unnerved her, obliterated the joy she'd taken in working magic once again. The kindest thing her kinswomen could do was kill her.

But Roskellys prided themselves on never being kind.

CHAPTER 2

Sean Weatherford pushed up from his desk. His body felt creaky and stiff, and he chided himself for not getting up every hour or so to walk around for a bit. He engaged in the same recriminations most mornings, but nothing ever changed. Magic ran through his veins like quicksilver. It took the place of even the most rigorous exercise routine—except when he first separated from his well-worn office chair. A snort burbled past his lips. He'd worked most of the night, but he enjoyed the dark hours. The bank was quiet, all but for the security guard, who poked his head in from time to time for a chat over a hot cuppa.

Sean was second in command over all the Druids in the United Kingdom, but he wasn't particularly fond of managing anything that didn't involve columns of numbers and methods of making money vanish from plain view. He hoped to hell his underutilized status among Druidry wasn't about to change. After centuries of bachelorhood, Arlen, the Arch Druid, had fallen in love—with a Roskelly witch of all people.

He'd asked Arlen straight out if he planned to follow his bride-to-be back to the States. Arlen had said no, but things like that could change.

He stretched his arms over his head, rotating his torso to get the kinks out. Katerina—Arlen's intended—was a lovely woman. Hell, she'd had no idea she was a witch until quite recently, so mercifully Arlen had gotten to her before she'd chosen dark magic. Not that she probably would have at this point in her life.

No. Those paths cut deep and were usually firmly rooted by the time a witch began to bleed.

He raked a hand through his thick, brown curls, aware his mind was wandering. Probably time to call it a night—or a morning. In any event, Arlen had reassured him he had no plans to step down from his post, which left Sean safe in his underling role.

Maybe. As he'd noted before, the best constructed plans could change. Katerina had family back in the States. Witches. Breath whistled through his teeth. He'd feel better once he laid eyes on Kat's living relatives. Her dead ones were piles of malevolent dogmeat, bouncing in and out of their crypts like eerie jack-in-the-boxes. He screwed his face into a frown and hoped the Druids would catch a break before the dearly departed Roskelly women chose to pay them another visit.

Unfortunately, wishing had never bought him much.

He'd step up to the plate if Arlen left or the witches rose from their crypts again, but it was far from his first choice. Snatching up his computer bag, phone, and tablet, he strode from his office and out into darkness with a brisk nod and wave at the guard as he passed beneath the main entrance. It might be seven in the morning, but Inverness wouldn't get light until past ten. Not in early January.

The bank had underground parking, but Sean always parked a few blocks away. It was almost the only exercise he got, and he guarded his half-hour strolls, maintaining them even in rotten weather. Maybe he'd stop by his favorite teashop on his way to the car. Get a nice pot of strong, black tea and a few pastries.

He turned hard right and detoured toward the bakery. He smelled it long before he saw it. Cinnamon, vanilla, butter, and the scents of eggs frying in grease. Maybe he'd get a breakfast sandwich in addition to his favorite cinnamon buns.

A dog barked from somewhere behind him, and a

raptor wheeled overhead. A nighthawk on its way home. Sean focused a small beam of magic and wished it good hunting. It angled its body and looked right at him, dipping a wing in thanks.

Even at this hour, traffic wound up and down the darkened streets.

Thirty minutes later, he emerged from the shop carrying a sack with his breakfast in one hand and a large cup of the fragrant black tea he preferred in the other. He'd employed the shoulder strap of his computer bag to secure the item around his chest. He stopped for a moment after leaving the shop and breathed deep.

Huffing out the breath, he set a course for his BMW sedan. Mornings should smell fresher. Not like petroleum products and sewers. He shrugged pragmatically. The air hadn't smelled particularly sweet a couple of centuries ago, either. Then it reeked of shit and unwashed bodies, with a patina of rotting teeth tossed into the mix. Now it smelled of pollution, manmade chemicals that were slowly killing the earth.

"Och. Not so slowly anymore," he muttered. A quick glance ahead told him his car hadn't been disturbed. Still sitting on four inflated tires. No broken glass. Crime had done nothing but escalate in Inverness, to the point the local police squad was hard-pressed to keep up with it. Out-of-control lawlessness was a strong argument for keeping his car beneath the bank, but then he'd miss his daily jaunts.

He grinned. Life was a series of trade-offs.

As he walked, he mapped out the remainder of his day. He'd go home to his remodeled castle, catch a few hours' sleep, and then show up for an engagement party at Arlen and Katerina's around suppertime. Afterward, he'd return to his recently vacated desk in a secluded corner of the Bank of Scotland's main Inverness branch.

Or perhaps he'd splurge and take the night off. The thought pleased him. The term workaholic had been coined long after he'd reached adulthood, but the concept fit him to a tee. His grin widened. No one had ever rebuked him for working too hard or too long in earlier times. Humans had grown soft, with an inflated sense of entitlement.

He sent a pulse of magic to open his car door. His hands were full, and it beat setting things down to dig for his keys. A small frisson of something that shouldn't be there brushed down his back. He stopped, magical senses activated, but whatever he'd sensed was so subtle, he wondered if he'd imagined it.

The open car door beckoned. He hurried forward, bending so he could situate the tea in the console. The wrongness shifted from subtle to a full-blown tide, hitting him from all sides.

Shit. Fuck. This was what came of being sloppy. Damn the twenty-first century all to hell. In earlier times, he'd never let his guard down. Many a night, he'd even slept warded.

Dark magic rolled over him in waves. Power stinking of Black Witches. He tried to turn, but he was trapped, half inside the car, half out. His legs refused to cooperate, and his heart ratcheted into triple-time rhythm. Tossing the bakery bag into the passenger seat to free his other hand, he kicked the doors to his power open.

The earth heard him, and strength flowed through his boot soles, infusing him with sufficient alchemy to defeat his enemies. Maybe. Calling for help was out of the question. No one was close enough to get here in time. Besides, why put anyone else at risk?

The air around him took on a glowing, glistening aspect, and he propelled his body backward. The magic he'd summoned allowed him to break through the part of the witch's enchantment that had robbed his legs of movement. Spinning quickly, and chanting like a lunatic, he faced an amorphous glob of pulsating blackness. It glittered and shaded to gray in spots as it swayed, forming a half circle that pinned him against his open car door.

Something that looked suspiciously like red-rimmed burning eyes popped up first in one spot, and then in another. Sean asked for more from the earth, and mini lightning bolts jetted from his fingertips. Where they connected with the darkness, they hissed and sputtered before being absorbed.

Sean's eyes widened. He'd just shot the thing chockful of destructive power. It should be on fire, or at least smoldering, but nothing had changed except the eerie eyes, which were more visible. He upped the ante, running wide open, and hit it with another volley.

Same results.

The witch stench had escalated to an absolute reek, but it didn't smell like the Roskelly witches had. They'd been dead, and this batch was very much alive. Where in the goddess's name had they come from? He'd thought Black Witchcraft long gone with the birth of the current century.

Aye, and good riddance to them with their stinking hex bags and dirty magical tricks.

Blasting through the dark blob wasn't going to happen, so he shuffled through possibilities. One was jumping into his car and gunning it. It wouldn't discourage whatever had targeted him, but at least he could lead the abomination into open country. Something like a distant drumbeat started, low at first, and then growing rapidly louder until it nearly deafened him. Along with its rhythm, the blackness grew wider and taller. Probably thicker too, but he didn't have that perspective.

He blasted the seething cushion again and again. Power rolled through him like high octane fuel, but the shuddering darkness drew closer, blocking out everything. Somehow it had even slithered between him and the BMW. He scanned the sky, but it was vanishing as well.

What would happen once he was completely boxed in?

He didn't want to find out but diving into his car wasn't an option any longer. He had to stand and fight. What he was doing wasn't working out terribly well.

He needed a new strategy.

The harsh taste of adrenaline coated his throat and tongue. He kept his hands extended, fingers flexed with power surging through them. It might not be effective, but he couldn't think of anything else to do. If he were going to teleport, he should have done it the moment he realized things weren't right. Out of all magics, that one had the greatest propensity to boomerang back at him. Its bite was vicious, and he didn't want to add to his problems.

"Arlen." He raised his mind voice and followed the single word with the Druids' war cry. A single ululating note that ran up and down the length of the scale. It wasn't telepathic, but Arlen would hear. So

would every Druid in a hundred-kilometer radius. Calling for assistance went against the grain, but if he didn't he was a dead man.

No mistaking malevolent intent. It whooped and hollered around him, carved into every drumbeat, every flash of those eldritch red eyes. Pressure built around him as the eerie cloud closed in. Where it touched him, it creeped him out. Oily and slimy, it left tracks he felt through his clothes. Paths that burned as if someone had painted him with liquid fire.

He wasn't a warrior, not in Arlen's vein at all. He was an academic, a seer, a sorcerer who dealt with prophecies.

"For fuck's sake, man up," he muttered. Breathing had become harder as the thing surrounded him. It must be eating up all the available air. He tightened his hold on his warding, but it didn't jump to his call as it had earlier. To his horror, he felt magic sluice back through his body and into the earth beneath his feet.

Bitter laughter rose. He didn't blame the earth. If he had a choice, he'd run as far and as fast as he could from the atrocity that had him in its clutches. He was panting now, gasping. His vision developed a grayish haze.

"Noooooooo." His scream sounded thin to his ears, but he cried out again, trading his outrage for another round of the Druids' war cry. He was going down, but goddamn it all to hell, he'd make the sick sonofabitch who'd targeted him sorry.

Reaching into his coat, he pulled out the dirk he always carried. Its bone handle protected him from its iron blade. He drove the blade into the black thing. Withdrew it and did it again. And again. Drumbeats roared through his skull. Black fluid gushed. Wherever it landed, fires erupted, but Sean didn't stop.

It might have been his twentieth thrust or his hundredth, but the slender bit of sky above him vanished, closing off both light and air. He'd been managing on nearly nothing before, but the total absence of oxygen made his head spin. Nausea gripped him as he tried desperately to remain on his feet. Clawing at his useless throat, he visualized air molecules, summoned them with his waning power.

It didn't work.

Shouts and calls echoed from somewhere close. Druid voices, crying out in Gaelic. He tried to hang on, but his boneless body slumped to the cobblestoned street.

Or what should have been a street. The moment he fell, everything changed. No more streets. No more BMW. No more Druids coming to his rescue. The good part was he could breathe again. The bad part was he was in the midst of a time portal not of his own making.

Where had the witches sent him?

"Doesn't matter," he answered himself. "I'll teleport back."

He winced. Smartass words. He had a feeling it might not be as simple as he assumed. Someone had gone to a whole pisspot of trouble to move him. That same someone would be invested in having him stay put.

His thoughts galvanized him into action. Time travel was scarcely a finely honed casting. At best, you ended up within a year or two of where you'd aimed. He did a quick assessment of his magical center, relieved beyond words he hadn't totally depleted his ability.

Taking care to be unobtrusive, he wound a few tendrils of power into the spell that had him in thrall. All he needed to do was push it slightly in one direction or the other, and he'd roll out in a spot his tormentors didn't expect. In the time it would take them to track him down, he'd be long gone.

"Long gone," he repeated through clenched teeth. "I shall be as elusive as the wind. Those fuckers won't trap me a second time."

He pushed harder with his magic, edging the spell closer to modern time. He had no idea where he was headed, but he wanted to avoid where he'd been last time. The early 1700s had been a bitch to live through, and not much of a picnic to visit, either. Not with Hunters running amok, murdering magic wielders with the full sanction of the Church.

The tunnel surrounding him took on a grayish hue. Wherever he was going, he'd be there soon. He readied power. In case he had to fight, or cast an obfuscation spell, the moment he emerged. With far less warning than he had with his own spells, this one frittered to nothing, leaving him suspended midair. He windmilled his arms and redirected the magic he had at the ready into a layer to cushion his precipitous descent.

At least he was by himself. Fields stretched in all directions, tilled land that suggested he was near a major town. He touched down and sank to a crouch. Anything to make himself less obtrusive.

At least he was still alive, a benefit that might not have much permanence if the spell's owner found him. He spread power in a rough arc, running a quick test, but nothing magical pinged back at him. His ragged breaths eased. He hadn't been at all sure his efforts to queer the spell would have the desired effect, but if someone was hot on his heels, they hadn't landed here.

Not yet, anyway.

Before the thought finished forming, he got his feet under him and loped toward a dilapidated hovel about a quarter kilometer distant. The neat fields, lying fallow for winter, looked as if they'd been tilled using the time-honored combination of man, horse, yoke, and plow. He took a moment and sniffed the air, analyzing it for chemicals and pollution residue.

Sean nodded to himself. Wherever he'd landed, it was before gasoline-powered engines were in common usage. He crafted a glamour to make himself less noticeable, trading his tailored suit and tie for tattered trousers, a shirt made from homespun, and a patched cloak. He couldn't make his polished loafers vanish, so he altered their appearance into a pair of scuffed boots.

If he was where he thought, no one of his ilk could have afforded boots, but it couldn't be helped. He hoped to hell the farmer he planned to grill for information wouldn't accuse him of theft and turn him in to the local constable.

Dawn streaked the clouds, turning them iridescent. Time travel never altered the season, so it was winter here too. Probably around ten in the morning. The sound of raised voices drew his attention. Something was transpiring on the far side of the hut. He slowed down and turned his magic to making certain he heard the exchange.

"Ye must come, right now," a man insisted.

"It 'tis truly a witch—and I doubt it is—ye have her in irons. What's the rush, mate?"

Sean rolled his eyes. Of course it would be men.

Women rarely offered opinions outside their homes. Now that he'd heard a snipped of Gaelic, he knew more or less where he was. Late 1800s. The speech pattern was close to its modern variation with only a few differences that were holdovers from the previous century.

Witches, eh? Was it possible his intrusion into the spell had derailed whoever was following him? For a long, delicious moment, he hoped so. Hoped the witch in question would swing from a gibbet.

Except they'd stopped torturing witches around 1865. He shrugged. A push here and there with judiciously applied magic might change a few minds.

"The rush, *mate*," voice one continued with a patronizing undertone, "is Father Abernathy specifically requested your presence."

"Aye, he did, did he? Why dinna ye say so at the front end?"

"I figured ye'd be so curious about yon witch, ye'd jump out of your breeks to hurry into Glasgow and see for yourself."

Glasgow. Solved the problem of where he'd landed. Now that he had both time and location nailed down, nothing stood in the way of following the men. The least he could do before heading back to his own time was ensure the pesky witch in irons met her doom. He edged closer until he could peer around the hut. A buckboard with a scrawny horse sat nearby.

Sean wound invisibility around himself. Seemed like a waste of magic after he'd gone to so much trouble building a credible glamour, but he didn't want to be seen.

One of the men cupped a hand around his mouth. "Brigid." Greasy dark hair fell around his dirt-streaked face, but his dark eyes shone with keen intelligence. A moderate level of power shimmered around him. Nothing earthshattering, but not bad for a human. No wonder the priest had summoned him to deal with a suspected witch.

Sean trolled through his memory banks. Hunters had fallen out of fashion in this time period, but the church still did its damnedest to stamp out anything magical.

A very pregnant woman spilled through the door, tangled red hair trailing around her patched frock. Her bare feet were streaked with dirt and muck. "Aye, Roger?"

"I'm going into the city with Donnell. Might not be back for a day or two."

Two naked red-headed toddlers, both girls, tottered through the door and stood next to their mother, burying grubby hands in her skirts.

"Doona be gone for much longer. The bairn's close to coming."

"Ye'll be fine." Roger dropped a hand on his wife's shoulder.

She shook her head and raised a set of bloodshot blue eyes to meet his dark gaze. "Nay. I fear not. I havena felt it move for a fortnight. I fear the child has died within me."

Donnel made a forked sign against evil.

Roger hauled off and slapped him across the face. "Ye will not point the demon's sign at my wife."

Donnell rubbed the red spot on his face but didn't raise a hand to fight back. Blonde curls fluffed around his head in an unbrushed riot. Upon closer scrutiny, Sean figured he wasn't much more than sixteen. His clothes weren't patches layered atop patches. Perhaps he worked for the local monastery, which would offer the advantage of regular meals and sturdier clothing.

"I'll be in the wagon," Donnell said sullenly.

"Be right there." Roger nodded. "Just need to get my kit."

"No need. I'll fetch it for you." Brigid turned and waddled back inside, her two children sticking to her like glue.

Sean eyed the wagon. He needed to sequester himself in the back. Was Roger's magic strong enough to detect his presence?

Guess I'm about to find out.

He gave his invisibility warding one last tweak and strode around the house, careful not to make any noise. Crossing to the opposite site of where Donnell sat in the wagon, he walked to the sloppily constructed wooden box and waited. He needed to time this just right. The wagon would sink under his weight, and that sinking had to coincide with Roger jumping onto the box next to Donnell.

Roger stood, arms crossed over his chest, waiting for his wife. He frowned and lifted his head, nostrils flaring as he scented the air.

Sean froze, did what he could to ensure his magic was contained. Another Druid would have known he was there, but Roger was no Druid.

"Here ye are, then." Brigid stopped in the doorway and tossed a cheaply tanned leather bag Roger's way. He caught it midair and turned toward the wagon, moving quickly.

Sean timed it as close as he could, vaulting over the wagon's rear staves just as Roger jumped onto the box.

Donnell didn't wait until he was settled. The whip whistled and the poor, old horse, who had one hoof in the glue factory, lurched forward. Roger stumbled but righted himself and sat heavily.

Sean settled into a crouch and hoped to hell they weren't too many miles out of town. For one thing, the horse wouldn't make it. For another, he had to remain absolutely still. The wagon didn't have anything as sophisticated as springs, and any movement on his part would reveal his presence.

It wasn't easy. The road was muddy and filled with rocks and ruts. All that would change with the advent of cars, but they weren't here yet.

Roger twisted his head from side to side. Sean didn't have to see his face to know his nostrils were still flared.

"Is aught wrong?" Donnell asked in a thin, nervous voice.

"Not sure. I sense something, but 'tis far from well-formed."

"Must be witch crud clinging to me. She tried to claw my eyes out."

"She did, eh?" Roger laughed and leaned closer to Donnell giving him a good sniff. "Aye, lad. 'Tis exactly what I sense."

Sean would have blown out a tense breath if he weren't committed to total silence. Things were working in his favor. He'd see that the witch in question ended up deader than dead. And then he'd find a way back to his rightful time.

CHAPTER 3

Few Hours Earlier

Liliana was so relieved when her spell developed wings, she spent her time in transit replaying precisely what she'd done. After all, she had to get back. If she was successful locating her mother, the return trip wouldn't be a problem, but there was no guarantee Gloria had stayed put. After all, she'd been "dead" for well over a decade. Closer to two, actually.

The blackness surrounding her developed gray edges. She steeled herself for just about anything. At least it would still be nighttime, which might offer some level of concealment. Had she constructed the spell properly? Would it truly spit her out in Glasgow?

"Guess I'm about to find out," she mumbled as the grayish edges developed streaks, turning lighter fast. She'd traveled to other times, but not since she was a curious teenager, drunk on magic and reveling in her burgeoning ability.

She gathered power, balancing it between her hands. Soon, very soon, the time-travel casting would fritter to smoke around her, and she had to be ready.

The distant clatter of horse hoofs on cobblestones reached her about the time she tumbled into a filthy alleyway, landing in a mud puddle that was probably teeming with an array of bacteria. She'd spent her years in medical school blitzing microbes with antibiotics. Something about seeing them under a high-powered microscope had forever altered her view of them as relatively benign.

An outraged howl from behind her was followed by, "Begone, devilspawn. Begone, I tell ye."

Oops. Goddamn it all to hell.

The man's deep voice spoke antiquated Scotch Gaelic, so at least she was in Scotland, and perhaps she'd hit close to her target timeframe.

She thought she'd done a fair job of masking her physical presence, but either she'd lost her touch—or someone else with magic of their own shared the narrow byway clotted with garbage. She breathed shallowly to cut the stench. Footsteps clacked— hobnailed boots hitting stone.

Did she have sufficient magic to convince whoever was hurtling toward her they'd never seen her? Once upon a time, maybe, but like any other unused skill, such a spell required time—and thought.

While nothing was amiss with her mind, she lacked the luxury of time to select just the right approach. One that might actually work, not dig her in deeper. She scrambled upright. Her cloak was soaked through where she'd fallen on it and smelled of rancid grease and piss.

If her situation hadn't been so precarious, she'd have laughed. Nothing like a tumble through a puddle to help her blend in with the locals. Turning, she saw not one but two clerics hurrying toward her, black robes flapping around them, heavy gold crosses suspended from their necks. Escape was out of the question. She might be able to outrun them, but the far end of the alley was blocked by a collection of crates. Even if she got that far, they'd nab her while she was climbing over and through the welter of wooden boxes.

Bowing her head, she crossed herself, cringing at the use of anything symbolizing those who'd persecuted witches. "Thank goodness," she murmured in what she hoped was passable Gaelic, keeping her gaze downcast. "Please. If ye could be so kind as to escort me to safety, I'd be forever in your debt." She threaded compulsion and believability into her words, and sucked in a tense breath, waiting. Would they fall for her gambit?

The men halted a couple of feet from her. Both were scrawny, and the one to her right was much shorter than her, but people had been smaller then. She felt the heat of their gaze as they looked her up and down. "Liar." The taller one spat the word.

She swallowed back a protest. Now was a time for silence. Women from this era didn't volunteer much, particularly not to strangers.

"Ye're being hasty, brother," the other monk said. Something sly ran beneath his words, but she couldn't quite tease it out.

Liliana didn't move. The surest path was making these men believe she was cowed by their presence. It didn't require much acting, since she was frightened to her bones. If it was truly the end of the nineteenth century, they wouldn't kill her for being a witch—assuming they figured that part out—but they might well throw her in a monastery dungeon, wrap her in iron chains, and leave her there to rot.

No judge. No jury. And certainly no possibility of appeal. No one would know where she was. The iron would erode her power sufficiently to nix any possibility of telepathy.

Panic threatened to swamp her. She pushed it aside. A clear head was essential. If she gave in to hysteria, she may as well drag her dirk out and plunge it into her own breast.

She'd lived through this time, been born into it, and she knew about the seamy underbelly of the church all too well. They'd only given up hunting witches in the 1940s because whoever had been Pope then finally outlawed it.

The men took a step closer. She resisted an urge to stand tall and stare them down. It would be an enormous mistake. Instead, she shrank into herself and kept staring at the ground.

"How is it ye come to be here?" The taller monk sneered showing rotten stumps of teeth.

"I was pushed from up there." She gestured above her head at one of the buildings. Up, but not too far up. Otherwise, she'd have to explain why she didn't have any broken bones.

"Ha. I doubt that." He leaned nearer, showering her with spittle.

Anger bubbled hot from her guts. How dare he spit on her? She scraped the back of one hand across her cheek, wiping the saliva away. "'Tis a sin to lie to a priest. I told ye true enough."

"Ye're requesting an escort?" The other monk raised a bushy black brow. Both he and his companion wore cowls, so all that was visible were their faces. Nothing warm or compassionate about these clerics. Suspicion thickened the air around them, turning their auras a dark, ugly gray.

"Aye, if ye'd be so kind. I'll not trouble ye further once I'm well away from this spot."

"No decent women are out by themselves at night." Brother Hasty smiled nastily. "We'll see ye to a place ye can wait out the dark hours."

She cast a furtive glance around her. Nowhere to hide. Nowhere to run. Not here. Maybe once they got out of the alley, she'd have more to work with. "That would be most appreciated," she mumbled.

"Follow me," Brother Hasty instructed.

"I'll be behind you," the other monk said.

Liliana got the picture. She'd be hemmed in from the front and the back. At least her heart wasn't thundering against her chest any longer. She'd been in worse spots, not many but a few. There'd be a way out, but she needed to be vigilant, not bypass any opportunities.

As she trudged forward, sandwiched between the men, she employed what she hoped was subtle magic to assess if they had any power of their own. It was remotely possible they'd happened past the alley at an inauspicious time.

Remotely.

More likely, they'd sensed expended magic as her spell first wound down, and then ejected her. The man in the lead didn't seem to be in any hurry, so she was exceedingly gentle as she probed. Fascinating. The man behind her was the one with power—not much, but enough to sense magic in others. The loudmouth in front of her was as bedrock human as they came.

They cleared the dank passageway. It opened onto an empty street. It couldn't be much past seven—or eight at the outside. Where was everyone? The monk had stated women weren't out and about on their own, but what about men? Surely shops remained open, and how about eating establishments?

Bells pealed, probably from a distant church. Liliana counted until she got to ten and the bells quieted. How could she have lost two entire hours? She refocused fast. It didn't matter what the hell time it was. What did was freeing herself from her captors.

Her gaze darted from side to side. She needed an opening, and then she'd run like a gazelle. She was better fed than either cleric. Probably stronger. But they were men, and that pesky Y chromosome always offered an edge. A lone carriage clopped by, a uniformed driver on the box and the curtains closed.

A policeman trotted by on the other side of the street. Swathed in a clan tartan, he sported a badge hung around his neck. A billy club swung by his side. For one wild moment, she considered screaming, but it wouldn't do any good. The monks would trump up a lie, say they'd apprehended her stealing from the collection plate or some such thing. Church justice was an entity unto itself. She'd always assumed local authorities were delighted to have help dealing with miscreants.

Even if she pitched a fit, said she was being held against her will, no one would believe her, and she would have thrown away whatever slender edge she might have. Right now, she was cooperating. Whether or not the monks doubted her story about being tossed from a window was inconsequential. She waited until both carriage and gendarme were well past them. A fast scan with magic told her no one else was coming either up or down the street.

She examined every side street, aware she couldn't be too picky. Yet she had to be careful not to end up trapped in a dead end. If the monks caught up with her, they'd be furious. Angry enough to beat her...

Piss on that. They'll rape me first.

The fear she'd shoved aside galloped back to the fore, closing in as one option after another flashed by. None of them were exactly right until a broad opening beckoned to her left. She'd always had solid instincts, and she didn't question this one.

Wheeling, she dodged the man behind her—the one with magic—and took off as fast as she could run. Aware even weak magic could stymie her escape, she ran in zigs and zags, doing her level best not to be predictable. She started to summon an invisibility spell, but the monk had seen right through her first one, and she needed every shred of energy at her disposal.

Liliana powered her flight with magic until her feet skimmed the ground. Maybe she should try to reverse the time-travel spell. Make a run for it. She assessed her magical well. It still had juice, but she'd have to slow down to craft any kind of complex spell. The men's footsteps pounded behind her, but they weren't closing the distance between them.

She'd surprised them, as she'd hoped to do, and a decent interval of maybe sixty feet lay between her and her captors. Why weren't they shouting? They had in the alley, but not now. For some reason, they didn't wish to draw attention to themselves.

She swallowed around a tight place in her throat and poured on the afterburners. They weren't making a ruckus because they aimed to kill her. Maybe they'd rape her first. Maybe they'd save that part for Act Two, but capture meant death.

"Mother!" She raised her telepathic voice. *"Goddammit. If you're here—"* Liliana stopped talking. Screeching for her mom had been dumber than dumb. If Gloria lived here, she flew beneath the radar. Probably no one beyond other witches knew what she was.

Even worse, Rhea might have heard her. Blood called to blood more efficiently than any communications mode ever invented. Rhea was still very much alive and would relish a showdown between Black Witchcraft and the two lone clerics panting somewhere behind her.

Once she'd polished off the monks, Rhea wouldn't just step away and wish Liliana safe travels back to the future. Oh hell, no. She'd expect gratitude—and compliance.

Never too late to embrace the dark side of magic.

A sour taste flooded Liliana's mouth, and she ran harder.

As she'd hoped, the street continued for blocks. Which way was it leading her? Even with a magical assist, she was growing winded. After another quarter mile, it sank in the men were herding her, not trying to catch up. Fear dug chilly fingers deep into her belly. Had they summoned aid? The one with magic probably had plenty for a spot of telepathy. She'd been so wrapped up in her own angst, she hadn't kept an eye out for power flowing from behind her.

Time for a different strategy. Next time she feinted right, she picked a likely cross street and bolted down it, looking for spots she could go to ground and shroud herself in an invisibility spell monk-boy couldn't penetrate. Her magic was far more robust than his.

Yeah, but he uses his more.

Quickly, before the men rounded the corner, she launched herself into another narrow, stinking side street. This time, she dove into a huge pile of rotting garbage, burying herself deep as she pulled magic like a crazy person. Escape was everything. She'd conceal herself so well, no one would sense anything lay beneath the slimy bits of bone, flesh, and decaying vegetables.

Bugs, mice, and rats crawled all over her, more than happy to trade munching on cold, dead shit for her warmth and flowing blood. Her physician-trained brain started to catalog all the diseases various vermin carried, but she shut it down fast, concentrating instead on her invisibility casting.

She was scared, but she couldn't afford to be sloppy. Once she'd sealed over the last chink in her shrouding, the cockroaches and rodents departed. She waited, barely breathing. If she'd fooled the rats, vicious, intransigent predators, maybe, just maybe, she'd elude the men.

She heard them now, cursing softly and blaming each other. Not sounding like men of god at all.

"Did ye call for Jakob?" one asked.

"Aye, 'twas the first thing I did when the poxy slut gave us the slip. He'll be here soon."

"Fine. We'll wait."

"Of course we'll wait. What? Did ye think we'd

run home, confess our sins, and be flogged for our trouble?"

If she hadn't been committed to absolute stillness, she'd have shaken her head. What kind of man put up with being whipped? Hell, what kind of religious organization turned everything human into a sin? You didn't even have to commit adultery. Simply thinking about it counted.

She hadn't forgotten how things were a hundred plus years ago. Not exactly. She'd been born in the States, and magic had a far more difficult time expressing itself in the New World. Clerics had never ruled with the iron hand they wielded in Europe or the UK. Consequently, witches and other magic-wielders had never been persecuted like they were here.

Should have thought about that before I came.

The rustle of boots and robes striding up and down the alleyway told her the men had no idea if she was even here. It was the last place they'd seen her, though, and by God, they weren't giving up any ground.

Rodents rooted in the trash all around her amid the sounds of squeaking, squealing, and chewing. It gave her the creeps, but at least they were leaving her alone. She fed power to her spell slowly, aware she had to conserve her ability.

How long before this Jakob showed up, anyway?

Doesn't matter. I'm here for the duration.

Endless nights sitting with patients, waiting while the ones who raged against the dying of the light finally released their hold on life, had taught her endurance. She'd do whatever it took, and then she'd leave.

Who am I kidding. I'll need to sleep—and eat. My magic won't be up for a return trip to the future for hours.

On that sobering note, she shut her eyes. One step at a time. At the moment, it wasn't at all clear the monks were ever going to vacate the alley.

A whoosh of potent power hit her broadside. Her eyes snapped open in time to hear a new voice, presumably Jakob, berating the other two in German accented Gaelic.

"Dolts! Ye're two great, stupid oafs," he railed. "She's right here. Dig."

The rats yowled in outrage as clumps of trash were shuffled this way and that.

Liliana threw caution aside and sprang to her feet. She'd meet this Jakob head on, not like a cringing ninny. She'd tried that route, and it hadn't bought her shit. Power shimmered around her as she stood, staring at a tall man with long, flowing blond hair. His monk's robes were immaculate, his gold cross studded with glowing gemstones.

"A Hunter, I presume?" She angled her head, regarding him through narrowed eyes.

A harsh smile played around the edges of his mouth. "Aye, and ye are a witch."

No percentage denying it. "Aye, but not the type ye believe me to be."

He rolled hazel eyes. "Since when is there more than a single iteration of witches?"

She made shooing motions with one hand. "Get on with things. If there's a cozy cell with my name on it, lead the way."

"Speaking of names"—he peered closely at her —"what might yours be?"

She squared her spine. "Liliana Roskelly."

His eyes widened; his nostrils flared. She had a moment of triumph at how she'd rattled him, but it didn't last long. Skinning his lips back into a snarl, he sashayed around behind her. One of the others handed him a length of rope, and he pulled her hands behind her, binding her wrists.

"What do ye plan to do with me?" she inquired. May as well know the worst up front. That way, she'd determine if there might maybe be a way out of this.

"Not for me to decide." Jakob eyed her as if she were part of the trash she'd just crawled out from under. 'These are modern times, slut. No one kens how dangerous your ilk are. Ye'll stand afore the bishop —and his mage. 'Tis for them to mete out punishment."

"But I've done naught wrong." She tilted her chin at a defiant angle.

"Creeping about, jumping through the very air like a wraith, is unnatural," the monk with weak power declared.

"I came from the future." She kept her gaze firmly fixed on him until he looked away.

"Pfft." Jakob wound another length of rope around her waist, dragging her forward. "Ye may be a witch, but ye're also mad."

Liliana jumped on it. "Aye, mad as a pregnant whore, mad as a cuckolded husband, mad as a Hunter whose gems lost their sparkle, mad as a—"

"Shut up!" Jakob hauled off and slapped her. Blood spurted from a split lip, but she grinned gamely at him.

"Do it some more, monk-boy. Been a while since I've had a holy man to play with."

He almost jerked her off her feet as he took off at a lope. After the initial shock, she kept up and broke out a bawdy drinking song. If she could convince them she was insane, they'd send her to an asylum—a place she might be able to escape from. No one wanted crazy people around. They hadn't figured out mental illness wasn't contagious, so they locked madwomen away.

And paid them very little heed.

She tossed her head back and sang,

"It were Happy Jack's undrinkable ale.

One mighty sup puts the wind in your sail.

The ale was a black as a night with no moon in December.

As bitter as a man who lost his pizzle in May.

As strong as six horses. As evil and wicked as Judas—"

The Hunter halted so abruptly she slammed into his back. "Enough," he growled. "If ye keep up that caterwauling, I'll rethink my orders. Ye could vanish into the sea, with no one the wiser. Do ye understand me, slut?"

"Yeah," she snarled back in English. Let the fucker make what he would of that. "I understand you fine."

He started forward again, and she let the rope extend to its full length before stumbling after him. Let them think her weak and crazy. She'd bide her time. Something would break for her.

It had to.

CHAPTER 4

Sean balanced on his haunches, compensating for the sway of the wagon. Town walls constructed of brick and stones came into view after about a quarter hour. Good thing. Every time the rickety wagon trundled over a rock or a pothole was nip and tuck. He considered sitting, but that would slow him down when it came time to exit the wagon's bed. He'd have to finesse jumping out of the cart much the same way he'd managed getting into it, which meant he wouldn't have a hell of a lot of time.

Donnell had mentioned a Father Abernathy. Sounded like a Catholic priest, but the man could be affiliated with anything from the Church of Scotland to the Scottish Episcopal Church. He probably wasn't a Calvinist since they didn't usually refer to their spiritual leaders as Father.

The wagon slowed at the town walls before a guard waved them through. Unlike during medieval times, the current walls were more for show than defense. Once they deteriorated sufficiently, they wouldn't be replaced. Apparently, Donnell and his wagon were known to the uniformed guard because he called out a greeting. The wagon rumbled beneath wooden arches in need of a coat of paint. After weaving through a series of progressively narrower streets, they turned onto a wide boulevard. The skies, which had been thick and gray, spewed rain.

Sean longed to pull his jacket over his head, but he didn't dare move. So far, Roger hadn't so much as looked back over a shoulder. There were worse things than getting wet. Being apprehended was one of them. He'd had time to think about why he'd been conveniently swept out of the way, and he didn't care much for the answer that jumped to the fore.

Witches all knew one another. He assumed their knowledge extended to the dead ones as well as their living relatives. He, Arlen, and a few other Druids had done a bang-up job alienating Rhea Roskelly, Katerina's great-great grandmother. The woman was dead, but it wasn't a showstopper, merely an inconvenience. She'd reached beyond her crypt to mobilize other Black Magic practitioners.

They were the group who'd jumped him. He offered up a small prayer Arlen and whoever else had ridden to his rescue had made hash out of the witches. There were ways to kill them so they remained dead, and it warmed him to think about every single one. Beheading was his personal favorite. Quick, clean, and permanent. Followed by a good dousing in mage fire.

From what he could piece together, a witch had died unexpectedly, leaving Katerina as the Roskellys' sole hope to produce progeny. That was when Rhea had upped the ante and kidnapped her great-great-granddaughter, dragging her backward in time to force her to pick up the family banner.

Rhea's motives were simple. If Katerina didn't hurry up and supply bairns, the thousand-year-old line of witches would die out. Katerina's mother and grandmother had told Rhea to piss up a rope. They were satisfied with White Witchcraft. Neither had any interest in Black Magic or in lapping up human misery to strengthen themselves.

Since Katerina didn't even know she was a witch, her kinswoman hadn't gotten very far, but that wasn't the important part. If witches from different families were banding together to weaken Druid ranks, it had to mean the Roskellys were planning another end run to capture Katerina.

Was he the only one they'd knocked out of the equation? Had they captured others? If so, where the hell were they? Or was the plan to scatter the lot of them hither-thither throughout time?

The wagon was definitely slowing. He readied himself to jump down. By far the easiest route would be for him to get out after Donnell and Roger had left, but he couldn't risk it. He needed to follow them, maybe through locked doors, into a place someone would probably notice expended power. The only magic that was safe at all was what he currently had himself shrouded with. Even with taking care nothing bled through his warding, Roger had sensed something. If Donnell hadn't piped up about being doused in witch spatterings, the sorcerer would have dug deeper.

Donnell turned the nag into a courtyard. High wooden gates swung shut behind them, seemingly on their own, but Roger must have nudged them with magic.

Fucking great. I'm locked in.

Not that a splash of magic wouldn't open the gates, but it would be damned difficult to avoid detection. Even if no one noticed his power, gates opening on their own would be sure to snare someone's attention. And not in a good way.

Sean set his jaw in a tight line. The smart thing

would have been to cast his own time spell and return to Inverness. Particularly in light of his suspicions about the Roskellys planning another attempt to snag Katerina.

Too late now. He'd set a course and had to see it through. He could lurk next to the gate and sneak through the next time it opened—or he could try to teleport and hope the burst of power didn't bring someone running. As long as he was here, though, he may as well retreat to Plan A, which was making sure the captured witch ended up dead. If she was hanged or burned—or beheaded—it would strip her of the residual power Rhea loved to tap into.

He smothered a nasty grin. Maybe the captured witch *was* Rhea. Wouldn't that be just perfect? Nothing like two birds with a single stone.

Donnell jumped down from the box. Sean readied himself. He'd missed an opportunity to match Donnell's egress. He couldn't afford to flub up Roger's. Keeping an eagle eye on the sorcerer, he noted the bunch of muscles that meant the man was preparing to jump.

Donnell was unhooking the horse from its traces, crooning to the nag and promising it an extra serving of oats.

"Stop that." Roger's irritation made for harsh

words. "Damned horse is on its last legs, and ye know it."

"Aye, but she's my friend."

A sour expression crossed Roger's craggy face. Gathering himself, he jumped to the ground. Sean was close behind, but maybe not quite close enough. The wagon rocked, canting toward the right rear, something that shouldn't have happened.

Roger hissed, turning slowly in a full circle, his dark eyes raking the courtyard.

Sean held his ground, standing stock-still behind the wagon. He was vulnerable, but if he let go of his warding, redirecting his magic to fight mode, he'd be even more defenseless. In the seconds it took to regroup, the sorcerer could bind him.

He may never have been much of a warrior, but he had a sound mind and was excellent at running probabilities.

Donnell looked up from cooing to the horse. "Damn. The rear wheel must have failed again. It's been in bad shape from the winter. I'll see it's replaced afore I drive ye home."

"Ye do that." Roger spat the words and stalked toward a small door cut into the side of an imposing stone building.

Sean had been so absorbed, first in his thoughts and

then in his efforts to exit the wagon unobtrusively, he hadn't taken a good look around. The wagon sat inside a stockade that looked like an Old West fort. Built of vertical logs lashed together at top and bottom, it was about twenty feet square and backed onto a four-story building made of stone and mortar. A stained-glass window suggested this was a church.

Made sense. He tried to reconstruct Glasgow from 130 years ago and decided this was like as not the Metropolitan Cathedral. Roger wasn't paying the wagon any further heed, so Sean hustled after him, staying close but not too close.

"Ye coming?" Roger called over a shoulder in Donnell's direction without breaking stride.

"Nay. I've had my fill of witches for a lifetime."

"As ye will." Roger grasped a metal latch and pulled the door open. It didn't appear to be either locked or warded in any way, so Sean afforded the other man a comfortable margin ahead of him. Easy enough to locate him once he was inside.

The smells of cedar, incense, and raw spirits wafted through the open door. He scooted through before it shut. No reason to freak Donnell out further. The boy had a compassionate streak. He'd named the old horse as a friend. It spoke well for him.

As Sean had figured, Roger left a path anyone with

a ten-year-old's grasp of magic could have followed. The lower level of the building rose around him, silent and menacing, but he only saw it that way because of his hatred for anything linked to religion.

The Church had sealed the Druids' fate by discrediting them. In truth, all the Church cared about were the offerings the townspeople left. Without followers or support, Druids had faded out of plain sight, become shadowy figures almost no one remembered.

A staircase rose ahead of him, steep and narrow. He thickened the magic around himself, intent on not having a squeaky step give him away. Roger's heavy tread made the risers bounce and protest. It didn't bode well for following him.

Except Roger was quite a way ahead. Sean willed the mage to remain focused on his upcoming confrontation with the witch and mounted the first step, keeping to the edges. The first half dozen risers went smoothly. Step number seven had a horizontal crack running from one side to the other. Skipping it was a long reach, but Sean risked a small magical boost, so he'd land silently.

Roger's footsteps didn't even slow down.

Sean grabbed his advantage with both hands and forged ahead. Still careful. Still quiet as he could manage, but he understood Roger's attention lay elsewhere. The other man was gearing up for his skirmish with the witch.

Roger wasn't a Hunter. He lacked both crucifix and gemstones. He had a family. How he'd ended up a pet lackey for Father Abernathy remained a mystery, but Sean had bigger fish to fry.

Like working surreptitiously from the sidelines to make sure justice was meted out. Once he was certain this was one witch who wouldn't rise to ride another day, he'd skedaddle out of the cathedral and get himself back home.

Twists. Turns. Corridors. More stairs. Finally, he landed on what must be the uppermost floor. Roger vanished through a stout wooden door at the end of a long hallway,

Sean blew out a long breath to steady his nerves. Roger would have his awareness focused on the witch. It offered Sean a bit of latitude. Not a huge amount, but he wasn't worried an errant breath would give him away. Whitewashed plaster walls rose around him, and a roughhewn wooden floor lay beneath his feet.

He walked to the door, intent on listening, but his luck—which had run fairly strong all day, if he didn't count being shanghaied earlier—held. The door was a Dutch affair. The upper half wasn't latched. As if trying to cooperate with his wishes, it swung slowly open, creaking on metal hinges.

"Do ye wish me to shut it?" an unfamiliar voice asked.

"Nay. She canna escape," Roger replied.

Sean positioned himself so he could see most of the room beyond the door. He swallowed back distaste as the torture chamber spread before him. A small, windowless space, it held a breaking wheel, a rack, a skull crusher, an impalement device, a knee splitter, and a Judas chair. Hanging from one wall were a breast ripper, scavenger's daughter, cat's paw, Scold's Bride, and crocodile shears. The latter a device for cutting off male genitals.

Dressed in spotless black vestments, a tall, thin old man with snow-white hair swung an incense ball back and forth. His dark eyes held cruelty. This churchman enjoyed meting out pain. Probably turned the old fucker on.

A woman was strapped to a chair by metal chains wrapped around her ankles and wrists. Long black hair spilled past her waist, and bruises covered one side of her face. A quick shot of magic told him all he needed to know. This woman was indeed a witch, and a Roskelly to boot.

Unfortunately, it wasn't Rhea, but he'd still be delighted when they lowered her onto the Judas chair, splitting her from her woman's parts upward. Well, maybe delighted was an overstatement. The woman was beautiful with a waiflike grace that tugged at his heart. Sean ripped his gaze away. Witches were tricky, and this one had no doubt spun what magic she could —given her iron manacles—to twist the outcome in a more favorable direction.

Roger kept his distance from the woman. Magic pulsed from him as he took her measure.

The churchman, presumably Father Abernathy, rolled his eyes. "Get on with it, Roger. I'll miss noon prayers."

Sean choked back an exclamation. How the hell did prayers and torture exist in the same universe?

"Witch!" Roger snapped his fingers.

A pair of emerald-green eyes snapped open before narrowing to slits. "You heard the man of God," she sneered. "Get on with it."

Shock ratcheted through Sean. The woman had spoken English. Modern English. *American* English. Where was she from? Certainly not 1890s Glasgow. Even if she was an expat from the States, her use of the mother tongue would sound different.

"Gaelic," Roger snarled.

"Why?" She tried to lift her hands but couldn't raise them more than a few inches before she ran up against the end of the chains.

"So I can hear your confession afore I burn you."

"Oh please." She pursed her mouth into a sour expression. "They quit burning witches at least thirty years back."

"How could ye possibly know that?" Roger demanded, looking thunderstruck.

"Because, as I've explained to the Marquis de Sade here"—she jerked her head toward the priest—"I'm from the future."

Roger darted forward and slapped the woman hard across her face. "Doona lie to me, witch."

She muffled a yelp. An uneven red spot added still more color to the bruising covering much of her face. "For Christ's fucking sake. I'm not lying. Test my words with your magic. I admit I'm a witch, but a pretty damned incompetent one. We have little use for magic where I live."

"Why are ye here?" Roger sounded genuinely curious.

"I came in search of a relative."

A cagey expression played over Roger's features. "Can ye lure him here?"

"Already covered that ground," the priest grunted. "She refused."

"It's a her, and why would I put anyone else at risk?" the woman demanded. "If you're going to kill me, get on with it."

Incredulity rocked Sean as he listened from the far side of the Dutch door. The witch had to be telling the truth about being from the future. Her clothing, shoes, speech, decent teeth that had obviously known modern dentistry, and even her haircut screamed she was a time-traveling refugee just like him.

Nay. Not exactly like me since she got here under her own power.

Roger cast a sidelong glance at the priest. "Why, precisely, did ye drag me from my verra pregnant wife's side? What were ye hoping I could add to this?"

"Do not question me," the priest shouted. "I do God's work." His face developed a blotchy aspect, and he paced faster, incense ball swinging like a mad thing.

"Naught for me to accomplish here." Roger shrugged, sidestepping the issue of what constituted God's work. "Aye, the woman is a witch, but she told you as much. Ye scarcely required my services. I'll be on my way. No need to send the boy and cart. I'll find my own way home."

"I dinna dismiss you."

"Ye dinna," Roger agreed sounding almost affable. "I dismissed myself." He spun on his heel and marched toward the door, dark hair falling around his shoulders.

Sean jumped to the side just in time to avoid Roger's burly form hurtling through the door. Father Abernathy didn't make any move to stop him.

Sean thought fast. His original plans to kill the witch himself, if it came down to it, had changed. A lot. This Roskelly was from America. From the future, but how far in the future? If she hailed from his time, it narrowed the field considerably. Insofar as he knew, the only living Roskelly witches were Katerina, her mother, and an aunt. Yet this witch had said she'd come to the 1890s to locate a relative. It had to mean more Roskellys remained on this side of the veil than he'd thought—if you dialed the clock back a hundred plus years.

Aye, but even if she hails from, say, the 1930s or 1940s, there'd be a far larger field of living witches to choose from. More than Katerina's mother and her aunt.

Undecided on a course of action, Sean watched the woman closely and sent threads of power outward, testing for the taint of dark power. The same innocence that had drawn him before illuminated her features, making her beautiful despite the yellowish-purple marks spread across her face.

Determined not to be fooled by her striking face and lissome body, he dug deeper, hunting for evil.

The priest ambled closer, still swinging his incense ball as he circled the witch.

She skinned her lips back from her teeth. "I know your kind."

"What does that mean?" he shot back in stilted English.

"You enjoy meting out pain, delight in chasing souls from suffering bodies."

He looked down his nose at her and reverted to Gaelic. "How could ye possibly know a thing like that?"

"I'm a doctor. A healer. I work with the dying, and I shepherd souls to the other side." She paused for emphasis. "Something about dabbling with souls leaves a mark. I see it carved into you, and you'd best fear your own death. The shades you tortured will make short work of you once you cross to the far side."

"Tripe." But the priest's steps had quickened. Apparently, the witch struck a nerve. "There's no such thing as doctors who only work with the dying."

"Not in this era," she agreed pleasantly. "But I'm from the twenty-first century. I agree, end of life care is a relatively new subspecialty, but it fits my magic and my *compassion*"—she emphasized that last word —"perfectly."

"Pah. I do God's work."

"Yeah. Keep telling yourself that, *Marquis*," she sneered.

The priest crooked two fingers into the sign against evil. "Ye willna call me that again."

She rolled her shoulders amid clanking metal. "I'll do as I please."

Sean grinned. He was starting to like the witch. She might be cornered, but she wasn't giving up. Even better, the taint from Black Magic was totally absent. This might be a Roskelly, but she hadn't signed on with the fold.

Sean was certain of it. She couldn't ward herself, not swathed in chains. And his examination had been thorough.

Sean inhaled sharply, playing possible scenarios to their predictable conclusions. Roger was long gone. No one else was anywhere near this floor of the cathedral. He could take the priest down easily, free the witch, and—

Aye, and then what?

Help her find her kinswoman, of course.

Pleased to have a plan in place, he edged to a slightly better position. He'd have to release his invisibility illusion, but if he played his cards right, he could do everything in the space of a few seconds. The priest had no magic, so it would be far easier than facing off against Roger.

He let magic build within him. The woman felt it. Her head snapped around looking right at where he stood on the far side of the door, but she kept silent.

She'd recognize the feel of his Druidic power. Hopefully, she'd welcome it.

He was on the edge of loosing his invisibility casting when a different sort of magic oozed through the stone walls, growing exponentially stronger. The priest was oblivious to enchantment sharpening the air until it glowed with points of iridescent light.

The manacled woman sat as straight as she could. A knowing smile wreathed her features, highlighting her loveliness despite the damaged, swollen side of her face.

"Wipe that devilspawn grin off your face," Father Abernathy sputtered about the time the air pulsed and formed a glittering gateway. The priest fell back a pace, clearly aiming for a bell pull chain to summon aid.

"Not so fast, Padre," a woman said in a high, clear voice. The shimmery, glistening air fell away, and a tall, regal witch stepped through. This one's hair was russet colored and arranged in an intricate corona of braids. Her eyes were the same blue-green as Katerina's.

"Devil's work." The priest tried for harsh, but his voice was high and thin.

"Nay," the manacled witch retorted. "We practice White Magic, not that I'd expect you to know the difference."

The newly arrived witch pointed in her direction. Power blossomed, and the manacles broke apart, clattering to the floor. The freed woman staggered upright. "Thanks, Mom."

The priest lunged toward the women. More power jetted from the redhead's hands, and he froze in his tracks. Sean recognized the casting. It would render the man blind and deaf—in addition to being paralyzed. He silently urged her to add to her spell, so those impediments would become permanent.

The witch angled her head to one side, possibly assessing if she'd poured sufficient magic into her spell to ravage the man. Nodding once, sharply, she wheeled until she faced her daughter. "Oberon's balls, child. What the hell are you about, coming here and flaunting magic?"

"Rhea's on the rampage. She dragged Kat backward in time, and she's not done." The woman squared her shoulders. "I need help, and there's no other way to reach you. Goddammit, Mother. Why couldn't you have retired to Beijing or Dubai? No one knew you there, either."

"Rhetorical questions, my dear." Her nose crinkled. "Why do you smell like you've been rummaging in a dumpster?"

"Because I hid in a heap of garbage, not that it did me any good. Can we get out of here?"

Sean had heard enough to understand these witches were Katerina's mother and grandmother,

Liliana and Gloria if he recalled their names correctly. It was past time to reveal himself, so he let his invisibility illusion slip at the same time as he said, "Ladies. Forgive me for—"

"Who in the fuck are you?" Liliana screeched and swung to face him, hands extended and magic crackling from her fingertips.

He tucked his hands behind him, so they'd understand he meant them no harm. "Sean Weatherford, Druid. I'm second in command over the British Isles. I work with Arlen, your daughter's intended."

Liliana furled her dark eyebrows. "You speak true, but it doesn't explain why you're here."

"Not by choice," he growled. "I was on my way back from work earlier today. Witches jumped me, forced me back in time." He took a deep breath and blew it out before continuing. "I inserted my own magic into the spell to knock it off kilter—lessen the odds of being set upon by the pack of witches who'd kidnapped me. It worked, and I came out in a field not far from Glasgow where I overheard two men discussing a witch. I was furious then, ready to make certain whoever the witch was swung from a gallows, so I made myself invisible and went along for the ride."

"Why didn't you kill me when you had a chance?" Liliana regarded him through slitted eyes.

"By then I'd determined you were a Roskelly, sure enough, but not of the Black Magic variety." He looked away from her direct gaze; it wasn't easy. He wanted to lose himself in her green eyes and never resurface. "I have a funny habit of not killing allies."

"Pfft. We can all sing 'Auld Lang Syne' later." Gloria looked from one to the other of them. "For now, we have to get out of here. Sooner or later, someone will come looking for the good padre."

"You mean the Gaelic version of the Marquis de Sade?" Liliana followed her words with a snort.

"Aye, he's quite the nasty piece of work," Gloria agreed. She focused her next words on Sean. "What are you going to do?"

It was a fair question. He should return to Inverness post haste, but an hour one way or the other wouldn't make much difference. "Will you be traveling to modern Inverness soon?"

"I will," Liliana said. "As soon as I've cleaned up. I'm hoping Mother agrees to accompany me. Since I managed to get myself captured almost immediately, it's clear my time-travel skills aren't in exactly tiptop shape."

"You knew that before you came in search of me," Gloria said dryly.

"Yup. Sure did, but I was desperate. Like I said,

why the fuck couldn't you have settled in some obscure geographic location where I wouldn't have had to—"

"Chiding me wastes both time and words." Gloria made a chopping motion. Magic built around her as she summoned a teleport spell. "Are ye in or out?" she asked Sean in Gaelic.

He didn't even have to consider before replying, "In." So he wouldn't sound too eager, or tip his hand that he'd have moved mountains to not leave Liliana's side, he added, "We can blend our magic. 'Twill make the return jaunt easier."

Gloria shot him a piercing look that made it clear she scarcely required his assistance. He was also pretty sure he wasn't fooling her about his true motives. Her teleport spell snapped him up. Moments later, cottage walls formed around them, revealing a well-appointed stone lodging. One room had been separated into sections with curtains.

Before the spell had fully dissipated, she hooked a hand beneath his arm and tugged hard. "Outside. My daughter needs privacy to bathe."

"Clothes?" Liliana called after them.

"In the oaken chest," Gloria yelled back. "Hot water is on the stove."

The cottage door slammed shut behind them. Sean hunkered beneath overhanging eaves to stay out of the rain. "You dragged me out here for a reason. What is it?" He eyed the elder Roskelly.

"Smart Druid. Tell me everything that has transpired with my granddaughter. Leave nothing out."

Relieved she hadn't hauled him out here to tell him to leave Liliana alone, Sean nodded and began at the beginning. "Katerina was in Scotland for a lecture tour. As you know, she's quite the well-known cultural anthropologist..."

CHAPTER 5

*L*iliana skinned out of her cloak. It had sustained the worst of things from her roll in rotting food scraps and rodent poop. Even now, hours later, it reeked so bad, it made her eyes water. Undecided whether to bundle it up and bring it back with her, she walked through gauzy curtains to the kitchen end of the cabin. It was decidedly warmer on this side of the curtain, courtesy of a huge, cast-iron stove.

It probably burned peat or coal. Wood was scarce in the northern part of the UK. Kneeling, she unlaced her boots and toed them off, followed by her stockings and long skirt. She draped the skirt over a convenient chair and removed her light jacket and tunic. A cloth square sat near a sink with a pump handle. She wetted it, starting with cold water to ease the ache in her jaw. It wasn't broken. Neither was her cheekbone.

She sent a thin thread of healing magic to repair her face as she worked on cleaning off the grime.

All in all, she'd been deucedly fortunate. Even if her mother hadn't shown up, the Druid—Sean—had been standing by. She'd felt his magic just before Gloria blasted through a gateway, overshadowing everything with her potent witch abilities.

She removed the lid from a large stock kettle and dipped her rag into blessedly warm water, drawing it over her body and rinsing it out in the sink before putting it back into the kettle. She'd dump the water once she was done, but this way it would last longer before it became too dirty to use.

Once she was done with her body, she bent over the kettle, wetting her hair and picking bits of disgusting debris out of it.

Liliana rolled her eyes. She'd lived through this era, taken plenty of sponge baths. Absent servants, heating sufficient water to fill the old metal bathing tubs was quite a task. Water at the bottom of the tub grew cold long before more could be heated, so full-immersion baths were never much better than tepid affairs.

She grabbed a towel and dried herself, blotting water from her hair, before putting her clothes back on. She'd leave the cloak here. Maybe her mother would have a way to direct magic to clean it. Failing that, it could benefit from a stint with lye soap in the galvanized washtub tipped against a far wall. Wool took forever to dry, though, in perpetually damp Scotland. So long, sometimes garments developed a distinctly moldy smell that never went away.

Liliana smothered half a smile. She expected the movement to hurt, but her face was healing. Thank the goddess for magic to speed things along. The smile snuck out anyway—along with a funny tense spot mid-chest. She'd been diverting herself, specifically so she wouldn't think about Sean. Such a pretty man with his head of curly brown hair and sparkling brown eyes that glinted with humor. He wasn't especially tall, but he moved with a lithe grace that reminded her of a jungle cat on the prowl. Unlike her with her rumpled, stained, filthy clothing, his looked as fresh as if he'd just stepped out of a gentleman's club.

His magic was strong, too. It had to be for him to hide his presence from her. Why had she sensed him when she did? Liliana narrowed her eyes in thought. She'd have to ask, but she was almost certain he'd been about to make a move. No other reason to reveal himself.

And then her mother had shown up.

Two saviors.

Her grin widened as she crouched to lace her tall

boots. Feeling a million times better, she straightened and walked back through the curtains. The small, neat-as-a-pin house brought memories flooding back. Her mother always had a place for everything, and she'd chided Liliana for not returning items where they belonged.

She started for the door to round up Gloria and Sean, but it swung open, and they marched inside, faces and fingers red from the cold and water dripping off their outerwear. Her mother rolled her shoulders back. "Good use of our time. You're clean, and I understand what we're up against."

Liliana glanced from Sean to Gloria. "Guess you two had quite the conversation."

"You might say that." Her mother's keen gaze swept the cabin before she hurried to an empty bookcase. A jot of magic brought a riot of books and scrolls into view. Liliana offered her mother points for keeping her source materials sequestered behind wards.

"Which of our relatives are nearby?" she asked, followed by, "Why have they left you alone?"

Gloria didn't even bother to look over a shoulder. "Who says they have?" she countered. "Rhea and her three sisters are a scourge. So much so, I was considering returning anyway. It's damnably inconvenient to hide behind warding, but if I let it slip, they descend on me like a pack of crows."

"What about their half dozen cousins?"

"Aye. They're here as well. Still very much alive, unfortunately." Gloria plucked several scrolls from her shelves, tossing them into a cloth sack.

"It isn't as if they can force you to become a convert." Liliana gritted her teeth, annoyed. Of all the witchy families, why the hell did she end up part of this one?

"Nay, but they alternate between showing up with tea and crumpets and setting traps that make me very careful whenever I set foot outside my door."

"Speaking of that," Sean cut in, "how'd you know your daughter was here?"

Gloria did turn around then and sent an incredulous look scudding his way. "Young man. Blood calls to its own. Do I appear weak magically?"

A muscle danced beneath one of Sean's eyes, but he replied, "Not at all, Ms. Roskelly," in a bland tone. Liliana thought he was done, but he was only resting up because he added, "About that young man part. You may be on shaky ground. Druids live at least as long as witches."

Liliana's mouth twitched, and she cut her gaze toward her mother. Gloria hated being corrected. Rather than the snappy sarcasm Liliana expected, though, Gloria turned back to her shelves, plucked three fat, black, leather-bound tomes, and added them to her bag. A wave of her hand and the shelves once again appeared empty of anything beyond a generous layer of dust.

"We should go," Gloria said, followed by, "Get your cloak, child."

"Erm. I thought I'd leave it here."

Gloria furled russet brows. "You did, eh? Think again. There's dry cleaning where we're going. No reason for me to squander magic cleaning that fetid thing. Or energy scrubbing it. You're scarcely ten anymore, daughter, and—"

"You can stop there." To avoid the remainder of Gloria's lecture, Liliana scooped up her discarded garment, folding it so the bad side was hidden. Once that was done, she swathed it with magic to cut the stench.

The corners of Sean's mouth curled in what was probably amusement, but he didn't make any cracks about her still kowtowing to her mother's orders. She wondered if he had a family. Her eyes widened. Oh hell, he probably had a wife. It wasn't as if he'd ridden through time to her aid.

He was pushed here, collateral damage from her dead ancestors who still had a stake in controlling Katerina. Or if not her, then her children. Liliana's blood ran cold. Her mother had been wise when she'd argued the merits of Liliana not producing any more Roskelly witches.

Smarter than me by a longshot.

Gloria leveled a knowing look her way. "Knowledge is often like that. Too little, too late."

"Christ, Mother. Will I ever be old enough to escape your jibes?"

"Probably not."

Liliana bit back a snarky reply, opting for information instead. "I have a question. The man who apprehended me was clearly a Hunter. I thought they'd all died out by now."

Gloria thinned her lips into a bitter line. "It's what they wanted us to think. They're ever so much more effective as stealth operatives."

Liliana shook a fist at the air. "Fuckers."

"Why should they change?" Gloria shrugged. "What they do works for them."

"Yeah, but not for us," Liliana replied sourly.

"I know you don't require my magic," Sean inserted, his voice rich as aged whiskey, "but I'm glad to contribute to our return spell."

"Where are we emerging?" Gloria asked.

"My house," Sean and Liliana said nearly in unison.

"Since the two of you don't know one another, or

didn't before today, which house is it?" Gloria asked as power built around her. "My vote would be for landing in Inverness, not California. That way, we'll be close enough to my granddaughter to do some good."

Liliana sucked in a tight breath. "I agree about being in Scotland, but I really need to stop by my home first, get a few things, and arrive across the Atlantic by airplane. Like a human, not a witch."

"Why?" Gloria's red brows were furled like flags. "What could possibly be so important you can't buy what you need in Inverness?"

"My grimoire." Liliana was hedging, but she wasn't looking forward to her promised soul-baring session with Katerina.

"Hogwash." Gloria's voice was flat. She released her magic, and the air turned shimmery with light as she stalked to Liliana and dropped a heavy hand atop her shoulder. Switching to Gaelic, she said, "Ye brought this on yourself. Ye insisted on keeping Katerina in the dark about her heritage. After ye insisted on birthing her." Her voice softened. "I ken ye thought the hens wouldna come home to roost, but now they have."

Liliana coughed and then cleared her throat. "Kat and I covered some of that ground on the phone, but Christ, Mother, I have to tell her about Warren. About how he died. She'll be devastated."

"Maybe." Gloria turned a hand palm up. "She's nearly forty, fully grown, successful in her own right. Give her a wee bit of credit. If she's angry about anything, it will be us not preparing her for an end run on Rhea's part."

A corner of Liliana's mouth twisted downward. "You always predicted Rhea would surface and make a play for Kat."

"And ye never believed me." Gloria made a rude snorting noise. "Should have stood ye a wager, daughter. I could have cleaned ye out."

"Can we hash this over once we're safely back in Inverness?" Sean asked, and then added, "I'll take care of guiding us to the proper spot." The clean, sweet scent of Druid magic rose from him, damp moorlands, heather, and gorse thickets, mixed with piquant undernotes.

Liliana breathed in his scent. It made her long for his arms around her, and the press of his chiseled mouth atop hers...

Stop. Just stop. What the hell is wrong with me?

Other than not being laid in years, nothing much, she answered herself.

To cover her discomfiture, she tossed her own power into the mix. It diverted her from longing for the Druid glistening with magic that painted him with an otherworldly splendor. Or from wondering what the sticky bits clinging to her fingertips were. Something dead and disgusting from her cloak, no doubt.

Gloria shepherded their magic, weaving it into a powerful shroud pulsing with enchantment. The mix of witch and Druid magics created a product more powerful than either by itself. Liliana seemed to recollect mingled power was exponentially stronger.

The walls of her mother's house fell away, replaced by the black nothingness of a time-travel passageway. Sandwiched between her mother's familiar magic and Sean's heady ability, a sense of exhilaration filled her. She recalled the incantation back in her basement, her stumbling efforts to kindle her spell.

This was far better. It pounded home how remiss she'd been about her power. No more. From now on, she'd give it the time and attention it deserved. Being a witch would come first.

It had to, or she'd be vulnerable next time Rhea showed up, which was unacceptable since she had to protect her daughter.

Ha! Kat looks to have done a fair job protecting herself, but at least she won't have to bail me out.

In far less time than she expected, the airless void between eras subsided, and a stately great room formed around them. Polished dark-wood furniture was arranged in small conversational groups atop authentic looking Oriental rugs. Silver, crystal, and bronze artifacts were scattered throughout the room, and paintings graced the walls.

Sean bowed low. "Welcome to my home."

"Looks more like a castle," Gloria noted.

"It is, but they're common as goose grass in the Highlands." Sean held out a hand. "If you turn loose of that cloak, I'll drop it in the laundry. Once it's had a turn through the washer, we'll spread it out to dry."

"Wouldn't hear of it," Liliana said.

He looked askance at her and switched to Gaelic. "Were ye planning to hang onto that stinking bit of wool for a long time, lass?"

Heat rose from her chest, sweeping over her head, until she was certain she had to be bright red. "Not sure I was planning anything," she mumbled and dropped her cloak into his outstretched hand.

"Back in short order," he said. "I need to contact Arlen. He and some of our order showed up this morning just afore I was removed from Inverness. He'll be searching for me, and I don't want him to waste any more magic than he already has."

Sean ran lightly from the room, vanishing through an archway at its end. Liliana sent what she hoped was an unobtrusive thread of magic outward. If he had a wife—or a girlfriend—elements of her essence would be detectable.

"Why didn't you come for me sooner?" Gloria

demanded, her question breaking into Liliana's concentration.

"Because I only just found out what had transpired." Liliana batted back defensiveness. "I don't live anywhere near here, remember? Once I discovered Rhea was on the loose, I ordered Kat to return home—without her Druid lover."

"Aye? And how'd that go?" Understated humor lined Gloria's words.

"About how you'd expect," Liliana retorted. "She refused." Turning, she faced her mother squarely. "We'd decided to keep her Roskelly heritage hidden, and—"

"No. You made that decision. I went along with it," Gloria corrected her.

"Regardless, I'll be breaking our pact. However it came to be. Damn it, Mother. Why am I always on the ragged edge of explaining myself with you?"

Gloria drew her brows together. "I don't know about 'always,' but in this instance you were wrong. You picked the easy path to smooth the short haul, regardless of consequences down the line. Did you truly think Rhea would roll over in her crypt and sleep the next few millennia away?"

"A witch can dream," Liliana mumbled.

"Aye, and hope as well, but your grandmother was a power to be reckoned with. Like an ill wind, she blows up shit, not caring who she hurts so long as her agenda moves forward." Gloria bent closer. "You paid her so little heed, you never even asked about the gap."

"Huh? What gap?" Liliana shook her head to clear her thoughts. It didn't work very well. Between being captured and used as a punching bag—never mind fearing for her life—her mind was a jumble.

"A generation sits betwixt me and Rhea. It's why she's Kat's great-great grandmother."

Liliana swallowed hard. "What happened to... whoever came between?"

"Yanna was my mother. She embraced Black Magic, hook, line, and sinker. Got a wee bit too enthusiastic and summoned a demon. It dragged her to Hell, and that was that." Gloria dusted her hands together.

Liliana curled her fingers around her mother's arm. "It appears I'm not the only one holding secrets from the next generation. All you ever told me when I asked about your mother was she'd died. What do you mean, that was that?"

"Never heard from her again. If Rhea is to be believed, Yanna became an indentured servant for evil. No one ever returns from Hell." A pinched look coated the outer corners of Gloria's eyes. "Made me all the more determined to stay as far as I could from dark power."

Pain for her mother's loss seared Liliana. "I'm sorry about your mother."

"Don't be. It's a waste of energy. What's done is done."

Sean hurried back through the archway. "We're about to have company. Arlen was relieved you're here—almost as pleased as he was to hear from me. And Katerina was ecstatic."

Liliana tried to read what was beneath his words, but couldn't figure it out, so she quirked a quizzical brow. "Of course he'd be concerned about you."

"Aye, but it runs deeper than that. I'm a perfect second for him because I have no interest in taking over as Arch Druid. Most seconds would be nipping at his heels after a few centuries."

"Makes sense," Liliana murmured.

"My granddaughter." Gloria leveled her gaze at Sean. "Will she accompany Arlen?"

Sean grinned, displaying very straight teeth nested in his strong, square jaw. "They're inseparable."

"Perfect. It will be good to lay eyes on her."

"And explain how it is you're not dead?" Liliana asked archly.

"She'll understand. Now she knows about her witchy blood."

Liliana sucked in a breath and blew it out, wishing she was as confident about her daughter's positive mental state as her mother seemed to be. "Who else is coming?"

"I'm not certain," Sean replied. "Probably half a dozen Druids, at least. Perhaps more. This morning was a direct attack on me, first time such a thing has happened to any of us in over a century. We'll be launching a war council to craft plans so none of us are caught unaware again."

"Are there other witches in the area?" Gloria asked.

Sean shook his head. "Not that I know of. Not before this morning, anyway. To be sure, there are Wicca practitioners and a few hedge witches with scarcely enough power to light a candle, but none with sufficient gifts to be of use."

"See?" Gloria elbowed Liliana. "I'm not the only one who fled modern times. Many of us used to live in this region."

"Mmph," Liliana mumbled, not wanting to argue. They had bigger problems.

"Why did you leave?" Curiosity lined Sean's question.

Gloria cocked her head to one side and transferred her direct gaze to him. "Do ye never tire of living in an era that discounts magic? Where ye canna practice your craft except in the dead of night?"

"Aye, I ken your meaning well enough," he replied, matching her Gaelic. "But the time ye chose scarcely accepts paranormal displays. Ye might have selected a few centuries earlier."

Gloria turned her hands palms up. "'Twas a difficult choice. Witches dinna fare well in the sixteen- or seventeen-hundreds. Earlier than that, and life was truly deficient in creature comforts."

A blast of power rocked Liliana. She turned in time to see the tall front doors fly open, admitting a string of people. Power shone from them, making her proud of the magic that kindled her blood. Liliana raced forward, searching the crowd for Katerina's flame-red hair.

"Mom!" Kat hurtled from the back of the crowd and into her arms.

Liliana held her tight and fought the thick place in her throat that meant tears were near the surface. "I love you, Katerina. I'm sorry. I should have—"

Kat reared back and shook her head. "None of that. You did what you thought was best for me. It's what parents do."

Gloria ran to where they stood and wrapped her arms around them from the side. "'Tis a wondrous thing to lay eyes on you again, granddaughter."

A warm laugh bubbled from Kat, and she smiled. "Lots of wondrous things here of late, Gran. And some pretty hideous ones as well. I'm just glad you're not dead."

"When did ye figure it out?" Gloria still spoke Gaelic. If Liliana's suspicions were spot on, her mother was too overcome with emotion to sort out English words.

"About the time it sank in I was a witch." Kat disentangled herself from both of them and yelled, "Arlen."

"Aye, darling." A tall, rangy man with shoulder-length black hair and shrewd dark eyes joined them. When he extended a hand, power shimmered around him. "'Tis a pleasure to meet your kinswomen. This batch, anyway."

"No kidding. The darker half of the family is a real downer." Liliana gripped his hand. When she let go, Gloria clasped it.

A shrill whistle was followed by Sean's voice. "Into the dining room, everyone. Let's unleash this war council."

"We'll get to know one another later." Arlen smiled. It lit his face from within, and Liliana understood why Kat had fallen hard for him. He was a striking man, but kindness shone from his eyes, and he looked at Kat as if she were the most precious gift in the world.

For a long, heartbreaking moment, she let herself think about Warren. He'd looked at her the same way—

until he understood he was dying because she was a witch. After that, he didn't look at her at all.

"Mom?" Katerina's blue-green gaze settled squarely on her.

"I'm fine," she replied brusquely and focused her next words at Arlen. "I'm guessing you know where the dining room is."

"I do, indeed. Come with me." He draped an arm around Kat.

Liliana and Gloria fell into step behind them.

Before they entered another oversized room, this one occupied by a long, polished oaken table that could seat two dozen, Gloria pulled her aside. "The past has no place here. If we do what we should have done years back, we'll banish Rhea and her bloody, fucking sisters to Hell."

"We've never been strong enough to tackle them," Liliana pointed out, adding, "Stay out of my mind. None of this is easy for me."

"I'll do what I believe necessary," her mother retorted. "We may not have been strong enough in the past to deal with Rhea, but now we have help." A feral smile carved into Gloria's face, turning her beauty harsh and menacing.

"Indeed," Liliana echoed. "Now we have help." She hoped it would be sufficient as she followed Gloria to a couple of empty seats. Goodness spilled from the Druids ranged around the table. Determination, too.

How many of them would die because they'd chosen to offer aid to the only three White Witch Roskellys in history?

Shit. Crap. What the unholy fuck is wrong with me? I need to mend my attitude.

Suspicion flared; she warded her mind. Either she was well beyond tired, or some of her less savory relatives were nearby, huddling in the ether to eavesdrop.

And planting hopelessness and despair for sport.

"Before we begin"—Liliana raised her voice to make sure everyone heard her—"ward this room."

"Sound suggestion." Arlen sent a pointed glance her way and asked, "Any particular reason?"

"Not sure, but we may well have unwanted company."

Gloria shot to her feet and spun in a circle, arms stretched outward and magic crackling from her fingertips. She set her mouth in a grim line. "Aye. They're out there, all right. Along with a handpicked cadre from the other side. Not especially close, but present nonetheless." She clapped Liliana on the shoulder before sitting again. "Good call, daughter."

Her eyes widened. Praise from her mother was such a rare event, it warmed her. Magic thickened as everyone shared power to create a solid ward. As it formed, developing a life of its own, at least the ugly bleakness lifted, and her thoughts were her own once again.

Thank all the gods and goddesses she'd guessed right. No one else had noticed anything amiss. Chilly tendrils wound around her spine. Rhea and her ilk might be dead, but it didn't make them any less dangerous.

Probably more so since the simple methods of killing wouldn't make a dent. Her mother had mentioned forcing Rhea and her sisters into Hell. Liliana had no idea what that might take, but if it required actually descending into Satan's realm, escape might prove impossible. The icy fingers stroking her spine grew colder still.

She forced her attention to Sean and Arlen. They'd begun talking, and she didn't want to miss anything.

"What happened after I was forcibly ejected from Inverness?" Sean asked.

"Unfortunately, not much," Arlen replied, his tone sour. "I swung my blade, beheaded one of the witches, and the rest scattered. I counted ten but there might have been more."

"Aye, along with a demon of some sort. I couldn't

identify it because I couldn't see it clearly," a woman with long, silver hair added.

"It had red eyes, right?" Sean angled his gaze toward the woman.

"Indeed. Eerie, penetrating, and blood red. You saw it too?"

"That I did, Morgan." He nodded grimly. "That I did."

CHAPTER 6

Sean did his job as Arlen's second, herding comments back to productive ground when they went astray. They'd been at it for at least two hours, and everyone was tired. His usual even-handed mood felt frayed, and he recognized they'd passed the point where they were accomplishing much.

He waited for a break in the action and said, "Arlen. A moment, please."

The other Druid turned to him. "Aye?" Annoyance scored his tone.

"We need sustenance. Rest."

A murmuring susurrus of assent swept around the table. A dozen Druids were here, along with the three witches. After Liliana's initial discovery that they were being stalked from the dark side of the spirit world, their warding seemed to have done the trick. The few times he'd felt beyond their protective barrier, he hadn't sensed anything untoward. His best guess was their uninvited guests had cashed in their chips and given up.

For now.

He swallowed a wry grin. Evil never had much of an attention span. It was one of many small things that could work in their favor—if they leveraged them properly.

"Seems everyone but me agrees with you." Arlen pursed his mouth into a thin line. "Recapping what we have so far, we will lure Rhea Roskelly and her sisters. Once they're nearby, we'll trap them with magic, kill them, and ensure a one-way trip to Hell before they recover sufficiently from their deathblows to fight back."

"More or less." Sean nodded, knowing it sounded far simpler than it would play out. "The part you didn't mention is we'll travel backward in time, to a place they're all still alive. They'll be far less trouble newly dead than they are right now."

He wasn't at all certain of that, but it sounded good.

"I still think you should use me as bait." Katerina sat taller.

"Not going to happen." Arlen stared daggers at his

wife-to-be. "Your magic is strong, but green and unproven."

"I resent that." Kat pushed to her feet, squaring off against him. "I did all right the second time Rhea kidnapped me. Even figured out how to summon power and escape my chains."

"Ha! More than I managed." Liliana cast a fond glance at her daughter. "But it would have been tough to do much of anything with that abominable priest breathing down my neck. What little power I could muster was focused on keeping myself away from his extraordinary collection of torture devices."

"Lil or I will be the bait," Gloria said firmly. "The draw is one more Roskelly to stir the cauldron—and produce children. Rhea won't care which of us it is."

"You don't know that," Kat argued. "So far, it's me she's had her sights set on."

"Only because your mother and I told her to fuck off—multiple times," Gloria shot back.

Sean recognized they'd hit an impasse. He scrambled out of his chair and made shooing motions. "Up and moving people. I'm headed for the kitchen. If anyone feels like helping me put food on plates, I'd be grateful for the help."

"Mind if I dredge through your spirits for a few likely bottles?" Arlen arched a brow.

Sean chuckled. "You've grown exceedingly polite.

You never used to ask. Must be trying to create a good impression for your almost-wife."

"Too late for that." Kat favored him with a grin and tucked a hand beneath Arlen's arm. Together, they strolled out a side door leading to one of the basements where Sean kept his liquor stores.

"I'll be upstairs in the library for a bit. There's lore I want to check on," Morgan said. Long, silvery hair floated around her slight form, and her dark eyes held a worried aspect. A librarian who dealt in antiquities, she was undisputed lore mistress for their Druid clan.

"I'll let you know when the food is ready," Sean called after her.

"Thanks. Or maybe just save me something." Her body developed a numinous aspect before she teleported one floor up.

One by one, the other Druids wandered out of the room.

"I can help with dishing something up," Liliana offered. "I'm a fair hand in the kitchen, and I'm starving, so I'm motivated to be quick about things."

Gloria clapped her on the back. "As you well know, I can burn water. I'll follow that Druid upstairs to the library." She patted the cloth sack slung over her shoulder. "She might be interested in the items I brought along. What's her name?"

"Morgan," Sean replied. "And the library is—"

"I'm sure I can locate it." Gloria trotted nimbly out of the room.

Turning to Liliana, Sean said, "You can just sit for a while if you'd prefer. You look beat."

"Thanks." She snorted. "Never tell a woman she looks trashed. I want to help. Means I'll get to eat that much faster."

"Follow me, then." He strode out of the dining room and turned hard left for the kitchens. Old castles like this one had several layers of food preparation areas, but he'd modernized them, along with the rest of the nineteenth century structure.

He did his best to conceal his pleasure at the prospect of having Liliana close to him, but maybe she was too tapped out to help herself to his thoughts. She really did look exhausted. Most of the bruising had left her face, but dark circles etched beneath her eyes. He wanted to care for her, shield her.

And he most certainly did not want to offer her up for bait any more than Arlen wanted Katerina to serve in that role. Sean reeled himself in. Arlen had a right to weigh in on Katerina's actions. He had less than none insofar as Liliana was concerned.

They barely knew one another.

The smile he'd been sitting on broke loose. No time like the present to remedy the barely knowing one another part. He shouldered a swinging door open, holding it and motioning her through.

Liliana marched past him. A sound that might have been approval whooshed from her, and she twisted from side to side taking in the stainless-steel appliance extravaganza, the marble counters, and the butcher block rolling tables scattered strategically throughout the generous space.

"Wow." She looked at him, speculation lining her face. "Were you a chef in a prior life?"

Sean chuckled. "Nay. A sucker in the current one is all. When I renovated the castle, I'm afraid I offered carte blanche to the designers and building crew. It seemed easier than scripting their every move."

Her generous mouth formed a soft smile. "I've always wanted a kitchen like this, but I'm too cheap to blow the kind of cash this must have taken."

"Why?" He held up a hand. "Never mind. It's none of my business."

"It's all right. When I grew up, resources were scarce, and I got into the habit of making do with the least I could get by with. Mother taught me early that any show of wealth would bring us unwanted attention, and maybe someone would look too closely and discover we were witches. It didn't help I earned most of my money as a healer, which meant I had to be very careful. If one person hovering at the brink of death made a miraculous recovery, no one thought much of it."

"Aye, but if ten of your patients bounced back, ye'd be suspect." Sean switched to Gaelic, a more natural language for him.

"Precisely."

"Ye told Father Abernathy ye were a doctor."

Liliana nodded. "I did, and 'tis true." She matched his Gaelic and rolled her eyes. "I finally lived long enough to find an era where women are allowed to take on more than menial, supporting roles. And I'd be a liar if I said I wasn't enjoying the hell out of it."

As she talked, he let his gaze rove over her. Nearly his height, she appeared strong and capable with a no-nonsense bearing that matched her chosen profession. Her green eyes shaded from clear emerald to a deeper moss color. Unbound, her midnight hair spilled to waist level, showcasing a high forehead and arched cheekbones that suggested Asian or Native blood.

"Do I pass?" she inquired archly.

His face grew warm. "Sorry. Dinna mean to stare." He stopped before blurting how stunning she was. Inserting action to cover his embarrassment, he crossed the room to an enormous stainless-steel cold box and opened the double doors.

She followed him and took things as he handed

them out, arranging them in a row on a counter. "What's in here?" She tapped a large plastic container.

"Chicken-and-wild-rice soup. Thought we'd heat it up and serve it with cold cuts, cheese, and bread."

Liliana swiped the back of one hand across her mouth. "Damn. Just hearing about food makes me salivate. Point me to the pans, and I'll start heating the soup."

They worked in a companionable silence for a few minutes—with him taking over watching the soup—before he felt gutsy enough to ask, "Where are you from originally?"

She glanced up from slicing cheese—and tossing every third or fourth piece into her mouth. "The States."

Surprise rocked him. He'd assumed she hailed from the UK. "How is it—?" He wasn't sure how to articulate the question.

Liliana nodded. "Mother moved to San Francisco as soon as she knew she was pregnant. Magic is weaker in the States, and she was determined to foil whatever plans Rhea had for me."

"What happened to your da?"

A shadow crossed Liliana's face, and she turned away from him, attacking the cheese with a vengeance. "Ouch. Damn it." The knife clattered to the counter, and she stuck a finger in her mouth.

He should stay on his own side of the kitchen tending the stock kettle where the soup was coming up to temperature. After a losing battle with "should," he hurried to her side. "Did ye hurt yourself? Can I do aught to help?"

"I'm fine." Her voice was muffled since her finger still resided firmly in her mouth. "I have healing magic. Remember?"

"I'm sorry. I..." He took a step back to give her space. "It's just I want to know more about you, and the only way I know how to do that is by asking questions. Didn't mean for it to come off as an interrogation."

She shook her head and twisted to face him, pulling her finger out of her mouth. Blood flowed freely, and she raised her other hand. Magic sparked from her fingertips, and the cut place began to draw itself together.

"Men don't fare so well in witchy circles."

"But some of your breed are male," he pointed out.

"Aye, mayhap so, but not in the Roskelly line."

He should keep his mouth shut, but the next question forced its way out. "What about male children? Surely ye produce them." Damn. He was back to speaking Gaelic. It revealed how uncomfortable he was.

She blew out a sad-sounding breath, and her shoulders slumped. "The male children never make it past the earliest part of gestation." He opened his mouth, but she waved him to silence. "Let me get through this. Won't take long. I don't know who my father was, only that he was human."

Another soul-crushing breath whooshed from her. Sean yearned to gather her close, soothe her, but remained where he stood. She wasn't asking for comfort, and he'd be damned if he'd do anything that made it appear he saw her as anything but strong and able to fight her own battles.

As if to corroborate his impression, pride shone from her eyes—along with determination and pain.

"Turns out Mother was the wise one." Liliana pursed her mouth into a moue. "Rhea never ferreted out who sired me. Meant he was safe enough." She shook her head. "I wasn't as careful. Times had changed since my birth in the 1860s. It took well over a century before I fell in love. Mother warned me. Told me to keep Warren a secret, but I was full of hubris and determined to show him off to the world. We were married in a huge, flashy ceremony with hundreds of guests—including my Roskelly kinswomen."

Her eyes sheened, but she kept on talking. "I ignored mother when she found out I was pregnant and ordered me to abort the child. Words passed between us. Unpleasant ones. She left, returned to her home in Nevada. And we didn't speak for months."

Sean took a step nearer, and then one more. He read most of the rest of the story in her heart and mind, and his soul ached for her. "How long afore Rhea made a move?" His voice was so harsh and flat, he scarcely recognized it.

"She muscled her way in right after I gave birth." Liliana shook her head. "Christ but I was a fool. I was so entranced with my baby, I never noticed her intent until it was too late."

"She fed off your husband, didn't she? Destroyed his immortal soul."

"Och aye. Until naught remained but a shell." Liliana spoke Gaelic now, too. "Katerina doesn't know. She believes her father died on a medical mission to Africa."

The tears glistening in Liliana's green eyes spilled over; she brushed them away, impatiently. A small smear of blood coated her cheek from her cut finger. "I have no excuses. None. I did what I thought was right to protect my daughter, and I ended up nearly signing her death warrant."

Sean couldn't stand not touching her. He wrapped a hand around her upper arm, offering what support he could. "Betimes, there are no right choices. Ye raised an independent woman, one who can think for herself, one who has excelled in her chosen field. Doona focus on what ye could have done differently. No matter how much we pick the past apart, we never change aught about it."

She leaned into his touch for the barest moment before pulling away. "Thanks, but if I'd told her the truth, she'd—"

"Ye have no way of knowing what changes ye'd have wrought." He regarded her. "One of my talents is scrying both past and future, although I'm careful where I look. The diverging path of one choice taken, while another is disregarded, is rarely worth the magic to pursue—unless ye're considering a future that has yet to occur."

Liliana fished in a pocket and drew out a handkerchief. She wiped her damp cheeks and blew her nose. "I'll be fine once I get through talking with my daughter. I promised her the truth, and I owe it to her."

The smell of almost scorching soup sent him galloping across the kitchen to shut the gas flame off. A quick stir reassured him nothing had burned. He pulled bowls out of a cupboard, spoons from a drawer, and set them all on a sideboard.

"Katerina will hear you out. I've found her to be levelheaded and accepting, given she didn't believe in magic until a verra short while ago."

Liliana winced. "Aye, and there 'tis. I used to worry her power would manifest and scare the daylights out of her, but years passed, and it never happened. As she grew older, I worried less." She smiled crookedly and stuffed the hankie back into her pocket. "Despite me eating half a pound of cheese, I've cut up enough cured meat and cheese to feed everyone. Ye mentioned bread?"

"Aye." He pulled a loaf from the freezer and blasted it with magic to thaw it. "Butter and preserves are behind me in the fridge."

She bustled about, placing items on the sideboard near the soup bowls. The haunted aspect still clung to her, but it wasn't as pervasive.

"Before we call everyone in here to serve themselves," she said in English, "I appreciate you listening to me. Other than Mother, I've not told anyone what happened with Warren. It's like this blotch on my soul that I couldn't save him. I snatched up my baby and drove as fast as I could to Mother once I understood Rhea had corrupted Warren. I'd have teleported, but I was worried it would hurt my newborn. Anyway, by the time Mom and I and a few more witches returned to my house, Warren was dead, and Rhea was gone."

She rolled her shoulders back. "It's a relief to be able to say all that out loud."

"Secrets, the hard ones, are like that, lass. They eat at you, rattle around like malevolent skeletons. 'Tis only once ye toss them out into the hard, cold light of the world that they stop tormenting you."

A ghost of a smile lit her wan features. "I like you, Sean Weatherford."

Warmth began in his belly and radiated outward at the compliment. "The feeling is mutual, Liliana Roskelly."

She grimaced. "Erm, I changed my last name to Curtis." She exhaled loudly. "One more stupid move on my part. As if separating myself from Roskelly would mean I wasn't a Black Witch anymore."

"Ye're not. Ye're a witch, sure as ye're standing here, but not of the dark magic variety."

"It's been quite a struggle sometimes." She narrowed her eyes. "The pull of that amount of power is heady, tough to resist."

"After a hundred fifty years, I'd say you can quit worrying about being seduced by the dark side." He was back to English now as well.

Arlen wandered into the kitchen with Katerina right behind him. "How's supper coming?"

"It's ready," Liliana announced. "Help yourselves, and I'll go make sure everyone knows."

Sean watched the gentle sway of her hips as she walked out of the kitchen. When he focused on Arlen and Kat, he expected them to be bent over the food, serving themselves. Instead, they were looking at him.

"What exactly were the two of you talking about?" Katerina asked.

Sean shrugged. "This and that. Your mum had a deucedly unpleasant time in Old Glasgow, but she's moving past it. Just needed someone to listen."

"What you said is true, but it's not everything"—Kat tilted her chin upward—"not by a longshot."

"Goddess preserve me from witches." Sean chuckled. Liliana's story was hers to tell, and hers alone. He wouldn't give her secrets away.

"There you are." Gloria dashed into the kitchen with Morgan in tow.

"Aye, here we are," Arlen agreed. "The question is why you were searching for us."

"We both agree," Morgan said a bit breathlessly. "What I mean by that is witch lore and Druid lore align on this particular topic."

"Which is?" Sean prodded. Morgan often got so spun out by ideas, her communication skills faltered.

"The two of you"—Gloria jabbed an index finger at Arlen and Kat—"must marry immediately. None of this waiting for the spring equinox. If we're to travel backward into the past, the marriage bond will protect you both, make it close to impossible for Rhea and her sisters to manipulate Katerina."

"So, I'm back on the menu as bait?" Kat grinned, clearly liking the idea.

"I don't think so." Arlen placed a protective arm around her, but she shrugged him off.

"We'll perform the ceremony tonight at sunset," Morgan announced. "It was the closest time to auspicious I could come up with."

"I'll officiate," Gloria said.

Arlen drew back. "Not that I don't appreciate your offer, but I would have a Druid. And our traditional wedding ceremony."

"Not going to happen—" Gloria began.

"Stop. Just stop." Katerina stalked to her grandmother. "We have a few hours. Work with Morgan and craft a ceremony that blends the best of both worlds." She looked over a shoulder at Sean. "You can help with that. You're who came up with our rings."

"Yes, ma'am." Sean snapped off a salute just before he broke out laughing. Kat was brassy and candid. He'd spoken the truth when he reassured Liliana she'd done a credible job raising her.

"I heard some of that." Liliana hustled into the kitchen and walked to Katerina's side. "I don't mean to darken your wedding day, but you and I are going to have that long overdue chat. There are things you need to know."

"Sure, Mom. Let's grab some food and find a quiet corner."

"Would you like me to be there?" Arlen asked.

"No," Liliana said firmly.

"It's all right." Kat patted Arlen's arm. "Mom and I really do need some alone time."

Sean wanted to draw Kat aside, tell her to go easy on her mum, but this wasn't his circus—or his monkeys. He liked Liliana, respected the hell out of her. Along with that respect came confidence she'd find her way through telling her daughter the truth.

Kat and Liliana walked slowly out of the kitchen, balancing bowls and plates.

Arlen cast a pointed glance his way. "You know something."

Sean nodded. "Aye, but ye'll not hear aught from me." He ladled soup into a bowl and picked up a spoon. "Looks as if we have a wedding to plan. Let's get to it, eh?"

"You're a good man." Gloria inclined her head his way.

"Why thank you, Madam Witch."

"Don't mention it, Druid."

Morgan buttered a slice of bread and made her way to a round table at the far end of the kitchen. "Here's as good a place as any to get that wedding nailed down."

Will and Krista wandered into the kitchen. Tall and lean with blond hair and frosty blue eyes, they looked like faery twins rather than mates. "Liliana mentioned the food was ready," Will said.

"To hell with food. What wedding?" Krista asked, looking at Morgan.

Sean grinned. Druids had exceptional hearing.

"Kat and I are getting married sooner rather than later," Arlen said, sounding pleased. "Once you've eaten, let everyone know."

"When?" Krista asked.

"Tonight," Sean replied.

"Oooh." Krista rubbed her hands together. "We'll need a dress, veil, wine..."

Will wove an arm around her waist. "Not your wedding, darling."

"But we'll all help with it, right?" Krista aimed her words at Arlen. "'Tisn't every day our Arch Druid takes a bride. Some of us figured you'd never marry."

"For now, eat." Sean added a smidgeon of compulsion to his words. It worked because Will and Krista headed for the food.

Sean took his soup and sat at the table next to Morgan and Gloria. He was tempted to use magic to listen in on Liliana and Kat, smooth things over if need be, but he restrained himself. He didn't want anything to stand in the way of absolute truth betwixt himself and Liliana, and she'd be both devastated and furious if he intervened.

He knew because he'd feel the same way if someone mucked around in his personal life without his permission.

Sean had never come close to being married, but he'd lived plenty long enough to see a whole lot of couples hit the skids because one or the other was a meddling ass.

"Sean!" Morgan's voice was sharp.

"Sorry. You have my undivided attention."

"Finally. All right, as I was saying, we'll open the ceremony with..."

*L*iliana unclasped hands starting to cramp from gripping her fingers together so hard. She and Kat had slipped into one of many side rooms, this one a small parlor with bay windows looking out on a generous pond choked with lily pads.

She'd been talking to Katerina for the better part an hour. Their food lay untouched on a small table off to one side.

"That's all the important parts," she said at last. "Thank you for not interrupting."

Katerina sat across from her on an overstuffed sofa, her blue-green eyes—Rhea's eyes in shading, but Kat's held warmth—liquid with pain. "Oh, Mom. I'm so very, very sorry."

Liliana held her daughter's direct gaze. "You have every right to be furious with me."

Kat shrugged. "How can I be angry when you did what you thought was best for me?" She hesitated a beat. "The few times Rhea showed up when I was very young, I used to wonder why she never stayed longer. Once I asked her."

Liliana grimaced. "Yeah, and what'd she say?"

"That you didn't like her."

"True enough. I did my damnedest to keep her away. Mom did too, but sometimes she'd slip through. Do you remember a time when you were nine and she—"

Kat held up a hand. "I do. Arlen coaxed that memory out or unlocked it or something. Rhea tried to turn me to dark magic."

"She damn near succeeded. If Mom hadn't been quick on the uptake, we'd have arrived too late. As it was, we barely got there in time. The spell was already simmering." She inhaled briskly. "After that, we used our first and last bit of dark enchantment to ensure Rhea never saw the light of day again."

"The asylum?"

Liliana nodded. "Getting her in was easy. Convincing the powers that be to keep her swathed in chains was far more difficult. We couldn't have accomplished it without borrowing from Black Magic." A shudder racked her. "I still feel dirty. It was such a relief when she died."

"Except death is kind of relative for witches."

"Ain't that the truth?" She held out her arms. Kat scooted across to the other sofa and burrowed into her embrace, hugging her back. Relief sluiced through Liliana, rich and heady. She stroked Kat's bright hair and her shoulders.

"I was so afraid I'd ruin your wedding day, but I couldn't not tell you, either. Sean said something about secrets festering, something I knew and pretty much ignored. I didn't want anything hidden to taint your marriage."

Katerina drew back. "I love you, Mom. My anger happened when I was a child. Rhea did something to make me long for her. I never truly got over it—until quite recently." She shuddered. "It didn't sink in that she had only one use for me until she dragged me back to the 1700s."

Liliana knitted her brows together. "That one, she never gave two shits for anyone but herself. And maintaining the Roskelly witch bloodline."

"Better late than never figuring it out. I can see why you kept quiet before. It's so convoluted and complicated."

"Exactly," Liliana agreed. "Even figuring out where to start became a challenge as the years passed. If I'd told you that you were a witch, you'd have chalked me up as having fallen prey to the mental illness you were certain ran in our family."

Kat snorted. "Hard to blame me. I needed an explanation, and it was the only one that made sense."

"To someone who doesn't believe in magic."

Kat smiled softly. "That would be most of the modern world." Liliana started to apologize again, but Kat shook her head. "If I'd known what I was, I'd like as not have never met Arlen. He's the best thing that's ever happened to me."

"Sure you're not angry with me? Not even a little bit?"

Katerina's face took on a wistful expression. "No. I'm more sad than anything. Losing Dad and feeling guilty and responsible for his death—and his parents' deaths too—was a huge burden. I'm sorry you had to carry it alone for so long."

"I wasn't exactly alone. Mom knew, but we got to a place where neither of us brought it up. Warren's death was my fault. Nothing I can do will ever change that, but he was a good man, Kat. He'd have loved you to pieces, been a wonderful father. He was so delighted I was pregnant..." Her voice ran down. She'd accomplished what she intended; no reason to wallow in regret.

"No more living in the past today. Not for me, and not for you, either."

She reached for their neglected food and handed a plate to her daughter. "Eat."

"Good idea." Kat layered salami atop cheese and popped both into her mouth, chewing and swallowing.

Liliana spooned cold soup into her mouth. It was delicious, tasting homemade. They concentrated on eating until nothing remained.

"I really do think I should be the bait." Katerina set her dish aside.

Liliana started to voice a blanket refusal, but something in Kat's eyes stopped her. "Why?"

Kat folded her hands together in her lap. "Simple. She knows you and Gran hate her. Anything you do to pretend otherwise won't fly. She'll see right through it. Her parting shot to me on my last jaunt into the past was she'd see me again."

While Liliana marshaled arguments, Kat kept on talking. "Arlen and Sean and most of the other Druids are old. It means they can travel to the past but can't remain long. Something about not having two of them in the same time period or something."

"I know about that part. It won't affect me, but it may well impact Mom."

"Hmmm, so long as you brought it up, how old are the two of you?" Kat leaned forward and angled her head to one side.

"I was born in the latter part of the 1860s, after the

Civil War ended. I never knew precisely how old Mother was, but my guess is she's at least fifty years older than me."

"How does that work?"

"How does what work?" Liliana asked, not understanding the question.

"Well, Gran faked her death and went to live in the past. What happens when people notice you're not aging like they are?"

"It depends. Mostly we fade out of sight and resurface elsewhere, although I admit it has grown far more difficult between DNA and identifiers like social and national security numbering systems. Not much that can't be smoothed over with magic, though."

"I assume you were going to get around to telling me about my, erm, unexpected longevity at some point?"

A corner of Liliana's mouth twisted upward. "I figured I had at least until you passed fifty to worry about it."

A knock rattled the door, not loud, but insistent. Liliana sent a jot of power outward and ran into Arlen's unmistakable energy.

"Come on it," Kat called.

He pushed the door open and walked through. "Everything all right in here?"

"Couldn't be better." Kat pushed to her feet and walked into his outstretched arms.

"Hey. It's bad luck for the bride and groom to see one another right before the ceremony." Liliana stood and then gathered the few dishes they'd brought into the parlor.

"Who made that rule?" Arlen's nostrils flared. "Not Druids. I need my blushing bride so we can practice our lines. I know the Druid ceremony, but Gloria added witch elements."

"Perfect. You worked things out." Kat beamed at him. "Since I'm not familiar with any ceremony beyond 'dearly beloved,' we need to get cracking. I'd hate to muff my lines."

"My little perfectionist." He kissed her forehead.

"I'll take these things back to the kitchen," Liliana said, wanting to escape before the desire swirling thickly around her daughter and Arlen ignited into something more than forehead kisses. "Is there a wardrobe where I can rummage for something to wear later?"

"Sure is," Arlen replied. "Once you leave the kitchen, take the first set of stairs up to the third floor. Sean has quite a collection of clothing from various eras. Many of his mum's garments and ones from a sister as well."

"Are they dead?" Liliana asked.

"Of course not. But nor do they live here anymore, either. I believe his mum is in South Africa, and his sister set up shop on one of the Polynesian Islands." Arlen chuckled. "Her parting comment was Druid societies be damned. If she never lived anywhere cold and damp again, it would be too soon."

Liliana laughed too. It was cleansing to let mirth run through her, and she felt lighter than she had in years. Since Warren's death, actually. She walked around Kat and Arlen and retraced her earlier steps to the kitchen, shouldering through the swinging door.

She was rinsing her plates in an enormous double stainless-steel sink when Sean strolled into the kitchen and to her side. His hair clung to his head in damp curls, and he'd changed clothes, so she guessed he'd come from a recent shower.

"Just leave those," he said. "I'll put them in the washer later. Speaking of which, I rescued your cloak and laid it across a drying rack hear a heat vent."

"Thanks. Maybe it'll be dry in a few days. That wool is a pretty tight weave."

"Won't take as long as all that. I added a wee bit of encouragement to the mix. I'll be surprised if it isn't wearable by tomorrow."

Liliana raked hair back from her face and turned away from the sink. "Arlen said you might have clothes I could borrow. I'd like to take a shower too. That sponge bath I had at Mother's cabin helped, but it wasn't a substitute for soap, shampoo, and oodles of hot water."

"Of course. Follow me, and I'll show you where a few chests are. Feel free to help yourself. I'll point you to a bedroom as well, one that has its own bath."

"Thank you. I appreciate it." She looked away. She was forever thanking him. There had to be some way she could turn into more than a liability, return his kindness to her.

He led the way down a different hall and up two flights of stairs. At the end of yet one more hallway, a door popped open, no doubt courtesy of his magic. She walked into a room set beneath the castle's eaves. Windows on two sides looked out onto the velvet dark of a cloudy, Scottish late afternoon. An inviting bed piled high with pillows and a plump duvet was tucked into a corner. Armoires and chests lined the other walls.

"There's clothing in all the cabinets. Bathroom is through that door at the far end." He stood near the hall door but didn't make any move to leave.

A sarcastic quip about whether he was planning to watch her disrobe died unspoken as she understood she didn't really want him to go. Something about his energy—solid and comforting—was like a balm. Soothing and enticing by turns.

"How'd it go with Kat?" he asked. "'Tisn't any of my affair, so feel free to tell me to take a hike."

"It kind of is your affair. You urged me to make a clean breast of things."

"And? Ye dinna answer me, not exactly."

He'd reverted to Gaelic. Maybe the witch's spell language created an illusion of safety. She crossed to where he stood and smiled softly. "It went better than my most optimistic expectations. You were absolutely correct about her."

Sean nodded. "I suspected as much. Besides, if there'd been teeth-gnashing or hair pulling or screeching, I'd have heard it even absent magic."

"You weren't listening in, were you?" Her hastily assembled comfort zone began to shred.

"Nay, lass. I wouldna do such a thing." He tipped an index finger beneath her chin and tilted her head, so she had to meet his gaze. "Hear truth in my words. I admit I considered lurking on the sidelines, but I care about you, and it felt disrespectful."

His words pinged cleanly off her magic. Heat from his fingertips was tempting, electric. When he cradled her head between his hands, she didn't draw away. Ever so gently, he closed his mouth over hers. The kiss was so sweet, so tender, and so brief, she longed for him to repeat it.

No one had kissed her on the lips since before

Warren's death. Trapped between guilt and failure, she hadn't wanted to risk another man to Rhea's wickedness. Refused to even consider it.

He stroked her cheek with his calloused palm. "I should have asked. This time I shall. May I kiss you, lassie?"

Her throat was too thick for words, and her heart was doing funny little flip-flops somewhere behind her breastbone. She nodded. He wrapped one arm behind her back and covered her mouth with his. The full length of his body pressed against hers, and she threaded her arms around him. They were of a height, and their bodies fit together perfectly.

He tasted sweet, like mead perhaps or scotch whiskey. The arm holding her against him tightened, and the swell of an erection pushed into her belly. Long-repressed sexuality surged, hot and primitive. She clutched handfuls of his shirt and opened her mouth to his tongue. Her nipples hardened where they pressed against his chest, and she delighted in sensation swirling through her.

It felt amazing to be in a man's arms after so long keeping to herself. He explored her mouth with his tongue, slow and lazily, trading kisses for suckles and bites that made her bite back. She poured her pent-up need, her soul, into that kiss, and her breath quickened.

He drew his hands down her back, leaving trails of

desire. When he gripped her ass, drawing her firmly against his erection, she writhed against it, wanting to be closer still. He ran a string of kisses across her cheekbone to her ear and down her neck to her collarbone.

A decidedly male noise, like a big cat purring, thrilled her, amped her embarrassingly apparent desire. She wanted to strip every inch of clothing off him, examine his body with her fingers and eyes and mouth. The thought of taking the pulsing length pushing into her belly into her mouth was intoxicating.

He lifted his lips from her neck and once again cradled her head between his hands. His dark eyes burned with an intensity that seared her to her bones. "Ye're an amazing woman, Liliana." He ran a thumb across one cheekbone and stroked hair that had fallen across her face out of the way.

"You're pretty incredible yourself." Her face heated from more than desire. What would happen next? Should she invite him to shower with her? It felt presumptuous, besides he'd already cleaned up. "I fear I'm desperately out of practice at this sort of thing."

A soft smile curved his well-formed, very kissable mouth. "As am I. I want you, but maybe what passed between us is enough for now."

The warmth suffusing her intensified. It didn't feel like enough.

"Lass." He tilted his head to capture her gaze. "I admit to sharing your thoughts just now. 'Tis been many a long year since I've been so drawn to a woman. We need time, ye and me. I could tip you across the bed, take you in a flurry of grappling and quick thrusts, but we deserve more than that."

She released her death grip on the fabric of his shirt and smoothed her hands across his back, loving the expanse of muscle stretched over bones. His scent rose around them, heady with the tang of damp moorlands and greenery. Musk mingled with heather, gorse, and rosemary. Her throat was dry, but she had to ask. "What do we deserve?"

A smile began in his eyes before spreading to his mouth. "If what I hope comes to bear, we deserve to spend our long lives together. 'Tis why we have time. Desire is like well-aged spirits, lass, all the better with waiting for them to come into their own."

Her eyes had widened when he'd said he wanted to be with her. Forever.

"Did you mean that?" she blurted.

"Not something I'd ever say in jest. I'll see you downstairs once ye've cleaned up." He kissed her, quick, hard, and sweet before turning and moving quickly through the door that shut behind him.

She blinked, staring at the space where he'd stood. The heat of him still lingered, and his scent was so thick it coated her tongue. She hadn't thought beyond a casual liaison, but he was offering more.

Far more.

She made her was to the bathroom, determined to bathe before she mucked around in the clothing chests. Her mind was a jumble, and her body on fire from his touch. Climbing over the rim of an old-fashioned clawfoot tub, she flipped the taps and directed the water to a showerhead attached to the wall. The tattoo of hot water on her nipples was exquisite.

Aware of her body in a way she hadn't been in a long time, she dipped a hand between her legs. Her labia were slick, swollen, slippery and she teased them, separating them to rub her distended nub. In her all-too-brief fantasy before orgasm shook her from head to toe, Sean was the one touching her. His fingers. His mouth. His cock taking her. She'd felt enough of it to know he was wonderfully endowed.

She shuddered against her fingertips, alive in a way that had eluded her before. Witches leveraged sex in ceremonies, harvesting its power, but she'd scarcely been a witch in the years since Warren's death.

As she stood, gasping and panting, legs quivering from her release, water pounding down on her, she vowed everything was going to change. She'd claim her magical heritage, revel in it as she had when she was young and flush with power. She might not ever return to her job. She'd used it as a panacea, so she didn't have to look too hard at everything she was running away from.

By the time she'd finished with soap, shampoo, and conditioner, she'd made up her mind. No matter what happened with Sean—and she hoped to hell he'd meant every word that crossed his lips—she was done pretending she was human.

Half a person. Half a woman. Barely a witch at all.

No more. From here on in, she'd be who she was born to be. No more compromises.

She turned off the water. Grabbing a towel, she wrapped it around her head and took another to dry her body. Hard tasks lay ahead. Maybe impossible ones. She might die in their attempt to corral Rhea and her rowdy sisters in Hell, but at least she was completely alive and facing whatever came next with everything she had.

Her mother's words about too little, too late mocked her. Thank the goddess knowledge, recognition, and acceptance had arrived in time. A riot of emotion swept through her: relief, joy, determination to be true to herself. Riding on resolve to not lose sight of her epiphany, she opened the nearest armoire and began rummaging through it.

Deep in her mind, the joyful cries of an owl on the hunt rose.

Liliana froze where she crouched, not believing what she'd heard. "Are you back?" she asked her familiar, too overwrought to manage telepathy.

"*I never went anywhere,*" it hooted.

She rocked back on her heels. "You did. I chased you away after Warren died. When I turned my back on magic and all its trappings."

More soft hoots. "*You only thought you did. I've always been as close as your summons, and today that call rang loud and clear.*"

When she closed her eyes, the bird's familiar black, gray, and amber plumage formed behind her lids. "Thank you for not giving up on me."

"*We're bonded. Giving up isn't in the rulebook.*"

"Someday, you'll have to scrounge up that rulebook. I'd like to read it."

The owl didn't answer, but she felt its presence, steady and reassuring, as she went back to her hunt for something festive enough to wear for her daughter's wedding.

CHAPTER 8

Sean floated down the hall and two flights of stairs. Leaving Liliana's side had been damned difficult but staying would have presented its own set of problems. They'd have made love, but once wouldn't have been nearly enough. If the fire burning between his legs—and in his heart—was any indicator, once he took her to bed, they wouldn't surface for weeks, maybe months.

He wanted their first time to be unique, memorable, not a rushed affair where she hiked her skirts and he unzipped his trousers. She was special. One of a kind. He'd spoken the truth when he said he hoped they'd spend their lives together. He'd almost asked her to marry him, suggested a double ceremony for tonight, but it was premature.

Particularly in light of everything she'd been through.

Between being captured almost the moment she set foot in Old Glasgow and girding herself for the tête-a-tête with Kat, Liliana had had a rough go of things. She needed breathing space to regain her equanimity.

And he needed to believe the attraction between them was real. Not an artifact of her reclaiming her power—something she'd used very little in the years since Rhea murdered her husband. He hoped what he'd felt as he held her in his arms was more than gratitude because he'd stood by her and been prepared to go to the mat to remove her from Father Abernathy's foul clutches.

Of course, he hadn't actually rescued her.

But I would have, and she knows it.

He hurried through one of many downstairs halls to his suite of rooms at its end, relieved he didn't run into anyone. Scots were a dour, disbelieving lot, and he sat at the far limit of that continuum. Spending his days surfing the seamy underbelly of high finance, money laundering, and offshore havens for cash hadn't improved his faith in human nature.

He reached to move his throbbing erection to a more comfortable position, but there wasn't one.

"What the fuck is wrong with me?" he muttered. What transpired upstairs had been pure and beautiful.

She'd melted against him, as hungry for him as he was for her. Why was he having such a hard time accepting she could care for him?

He replayed every moment, every touch. The hard peaks of her breasts pressing into his chest. The quickening of breath and heart as she held him tight. After his declaration of wanting to spend their lives together, she hadn't pulled out of his arms. Hadn't run screaming down the hall. Hadn't told him he was daft, that they barely knew one another. Nay. She'd asked if he meant it.

She wouldn't have bothered with the question if his answer weren't important to her.

He batted at his unruly appendage again, but it wasn't in the mood for retreat. Years had passed since he'd bothered with the one-night stands that peppered his memory. When he was so aroused he couldn't see straight, he'd found women—usually professionals because it was so much easier with them—and slaked his need. It had kept him going for another few months.

For some reason even that became too much trouble, and he had no idea how long had passed since his last liaison. Maybe a year, or as much as two. His cock was giving him hell, and he didn't blame it.

"*Sean!*" rang in his mind.

Something about Arlen's summons held an urgent

note, far more serious than if he were simply hunting Sean's whereabouts.

"*Aye.*"

"*Get out here. Now.*"

Sean didn't waste time asking where. He'd figure it out soon enough. At least his cock started to deflate before he left his rooms at a run, drawing warding around himself as he sprinted for the castle's common areas.

The sound of raised voices reached him almost immediately, and he recognized various spells, all iterations of incantations meant to stymie dark power.

Goddess damn it all to hell.

Were they under attack?

How in the fuck had that happened?

His castle was thoroughly warded, impregnable. Or so he'd convinced himself.

A deep, rolling roar filled his ears. The structure, its stones and mortar laced with Druid power, shuddered around him. Its fortifications were being breached, and the castle wasn't happy about it. He skidded around the last corner and into the great room. The ripping, tearing, crashing intensified until he clapped his hands over his ears. Pain ratcheted through his head, but his eardrums didn't rupture.

Why wasn't his warding keeping the horrific noise at bay?

After reaching a discordant crescendo, the noise was joined by a long gash in the ether at the far end of the room. Windows shattered, and an elaborate candelabra chandelier crashed to the floor amid millions of crystal shards. The rip grew longer. Blood-red scaled claws reached through, grasping one side and pushing it open wider. The fissure creaked and groaned like rusty chains scraping against each other, as it expanded.

Sean forgot about his painful ears and extended his arms. Magic sparked from his fingertips, and he sent it hurtling straight at the crack. Arlen's voice, hoarse and firm with command, broke through his damaged hearing.

"We have to close that thing. Now."

"State the obvious, why don't you?" Sean muttered. Even a magical neophyte could imagine what would happen if the gateway opened fully. The ruby talons punched through, followed by an oversized arm covered in shiny black scales.

What the hell was it?

Possibilities careened through his mind, but Sean shut them all down. He didn't need to see the rest of the monster to know its presence on Earth would be disastrous. Apparently, the dead Roskelly women had been busy scaring up help from Hell's denizens.

Arlen motioned the Druids into a line. Good plan

since it would maximize their power. A second clawed hand had joined the first, and the intruder grasped both sides of the fissure, levering it apart.

Harsh, strident cries ripped through the castle. Raptors, but how the hell did something like that get inside. Frantic, he diverted a thread of magic to see if a second breach had occurred—one out of their immediate vicinity. Before he'd gotten very far, an enormous golden owl with shining amber eyes winged down the stairwell with a dusky black raven right behind it.

Liliana and Gloria ran beneath the birds. The power he already had deployed revealed shiny multihued streamers flowing between the witches and the birds. Understanding slammed home. Familiars. The birds had to be the women's familiars. He'd read about such things, but never seen one before.

"What the hell?" Katerina screeched, pointing at the birds.

"They're on our team," Arlen yelled back.

Leaving his side, Kat loped to a spot between her mother and grandmother. "I want one of those," she announced before the rest of her words were drowned out by the demon's guttural shouts.

Raven and owl converged on the black-scaled arms that had worked their way through the fissure to elbow level. Hovering, wings extended, they pecked at the scales and talons. Black blood spurted, but the wounds didn't slow the thing down.

A hideous groan was followed by ripping, tearing, and shredding as the demon, motivated by pain and fury, pushed its upper body through the crack. Jagged edges cut into its scaled hide, and it roared and bellowed until plaster cascaded from the walls.

More windows blew inward.

The creature's head was enormous, twice as big as a human skull. Curling red horns rose from a low forehead. Patches of reddish hair dotted its scalp. Three spinning yellow eyes canted at crazy angles. But the worst part was its mouth. A huge, gaping maw, it displayed triple rows of discolored teeth. Teeth that had bits of red clinging to them. No doubt detritus from whatever it had fed on last.

Judging from its torso, also coated in interlocking black scales, it had to be at least eight or nine feet tall.

Sean had cut the flow of his power to avoid hitting the birds. The raptors tag-teamed their offensive. One would fly around the back of the thing's head, pecking at exposed flesh. As it heckled the offender, the other bird drove its beak into anything handy.

Intelligence wasn't high on the demon's list of attributes because the birds repeated their diversionary tactics over and over, and the creature went for the bait every single time. Sean took stock. For the moment, they were holding their own, but all the demon had to do was step aside and all manner of atrocities could spill through the opening. Whether it led to Hell or a borderworld or some other point in time didn't matter. Earth's integrity was threatened. They had to drive the demon back to where he came from—and seal up the crack—before something else saw opportunity and grabbed it with both clawed hands.

The witches joined the line of Druids, power flowing from their outstretched hands. *"We're stronger joined,"* Gloria reminded them.

"Here's the plan." Liliana's telepathy overlapped her mother's. *"Focus all our magic at that hole at the top of the crack. Force it shut. That should make the motherfucker panic. While he's thrashing around, my owl should be able to put out one of his eyes."*

"Or my raven," Gloria tossed in.

Arlen didn't insert his own strategy, didn't remind them he was the ranking magic-wielder in the group. It told Sean how rattled he was. Druids hadn't been targeted by a Hell-horde in centuries. Probably never since Arlen took over as Arch Druid.

He opened his magic, mixing it with the witches' enchantment. He'd expected the power pulsing from the group to brighten, but it turned into an absolute lightshow of untapped, raw energy.

Even the demon, dull-witted as he appeared,

noticed and roared his dismay. The birds, clearly in some type of communication with the witches, flew lower, pecking at the demon's hands.

Once he was confident the raptors would stay out of the line of fire, Sean let power flow, homing in on the two-foot opening above the abomination's half-bald head. Flames, burning bright with their combined power, and scented with clean, pure magic, ignited along the edges of the gap. It turned liquid, flowing together. Sean wanted to cheer but couldn't spare energy for anything beyond step one in ridding themselves of the intruder.

The demon craned its neck at an unnatural angle, shrieking rage and imprecations in a language Sean had never heard. It gripped the sides of the crack, not trying to force it open, but in an attempt to retreat through an opening that was now too small to do anything but crush the breath out of its scaled chest.

As it thrashed and writhed, the owl made a strafing pass. At the last moment, it twisted its head and thrust its beak into one of the demon's eyes. Black ichor spewed, coating its golden feathers, but it rose into the air, screeching a victory cry.

The streamer linking it to Liliana brightened and pulsed, and its feathers turned pure gold again.

While the demon had one clawed hand clapped over its wounded eye, the raven did its own strafing run, effectively putting out the other one. Joining the owl, it flew in excited circles well out of the demon's reach. Gloria sent a lavish string of praise in Gaelic, aimed at both familiars.

The demon's stench intensified. Before it merely stank of rotten meat, but now the rank odors of death and decay joined it. Not new death, but death where decomposition had gained the upper hand, acrid and cloying. Sean switched to mouth breathing to lessen the reek.

The fire kindled from their spell oozed downward. Wherever it touched the demon, smoke curled upward, and raw, red patches formed when scales disintegrated to sludge. Desperate, blind, and on fire, the demon curled its talons around both edges of the fissure and gave a mighty heave. A crack as loud as an automatic weapon report filled the room. The opening gave momentarily, and the demon threw himself backward, leaving a black, gaping hole.

"Hurry!" Arlen raced forward, magic blasting from his fingertips.

Sean and the others joined him. Once they were right next to the jagged cavity in the ether, an abyss that should never have been there, they peppered it with magic to seal it while the birds circled overhead cawing encouragement.

Maybe because they were righting an offense

against nature, things moved fast. Between one breath and the next, the crack's uneven edges faded together. The air smoothed over as if the opening had never existed.

Power crackled as they sheathed their excess enchantment, turning the air hot and bubbly. Sean was relieved they hadn't blown through every scrap of magic during the battle. Who knew what might happen next, and they couldn't afford to be defenseless. He scanned the formerly pristine great room and gave himself a sharp mental shake. The lovely antiques he was so fond of—many of which lay smashed to bits on the floor—didn't matter a twit. What did was that all of them were safe.

He hoped the demon had no way to regenerate itself. That it was permanently scarred and blind. It might serve as an impediment for the next horror-show fucker the Roskellys cooked up to torment them.

The owl perched briefly on Liliana's shoulder before shimmering to nothingness. Perhaps more gregarious in nature, the raven was still flying around the room cawing.

"Get back here," Gloria ordered in Gaelic.

The bird flew close but veered away at the last moment.

"It's happy to be free," Liliana said. "Let it fly a bit."

Katerina turned so she faced both her kinswomen. "What are those? Where can I get one?"

Arlen joined her. "They're witch familiars, *mo croix*. As to how ye lure your own, I have no idea."

"We'll work on it." Gloria dropped a hand onto Kat's shoulder.

"The familiars are kind of a consolation prize for foregoing the Siren call of Black Magic," Liliana murmured.

"Any other perks I missed out on not knowing I was a witch?" Katerina set her mouth in a tight line.

Liliana leveled a pointed look her way. "Nope. Not a one."

"Have ye altered any of the protections around this castle?" Arlen asked Sean, still speaking Gaelic.

Sean shook his head. "My first thought was how the hell anything had gotten through."

With a final caw, the raven settled on Gloria's shoulder before shimmering into motes of dark, shiny magic that almost matched its feathers.

"Where do they go?" Katerina asked. "Why haven't I ever seen either one of them before?"

Gloria still had her hand on Kat's shoulder. "I will answer those two questions, but no more. We have more important issues than your curiosity. The familiars exist on a separate plane. They're always in our minds, if we chose to accept their presence." A sharp look winged Liliana's way. "Our magic powers their physical forms."

"You never saw the birds before," Liliana spoke up, "because Mother and I agreed to conceal your witch heritage."

"Your idea, not mine." Gloria's tone was brisk.

Creaking and clanking told Sean the house was putting itself to rights. Some items, like the broken chandeliers, would need to be swept up and tossed, but the castle's structural elements were self-sustaining.

"If my castle isn't safe," Sean spoke slowly, weighing his words, "then none of our other homes are, either."

"The caves on the islands will be," Arlen said. "They were constructed with blessings from Danu herself."

"Are you suggesting we all move out to the Orkneys?" Morgan asked, sounding nonplussed.

"Of course not." Arlen reverted to English.

"What today's attack tells me," Liliana said, "is the sooner we put our strategy into play the better. Rhea is behind this. She's furious Kat gave her the slip—twice."

"And she's gunning for bear," Sean muttered.

Amid the tinkle of glass, the broken windows mended. Dark spots from demon ichor first smoldered, and then burned with a sticky, greasy smoke before disappearing.

"See. There it is," Katerina said.

"There what is?" Liliana asked her daughter.

"She's furious with me. Not you. Not Gram. Me. If I show up, proverbial hat in hand, and tell her I've had a taste of dark power and I'm ready to claim it, she'll believe me. She'll cook up that cauldron thing she started when I was nine. It's not an instant process. While she's adding rattlesnake blood and eye of newt—or whatever it is we use—you can move in and escort her to Hell."

"No," Arlen thundered.

Sean tapped his upper arm. "Lass has a point." He kept his words quiet, without inflection.

"I don't care. 'Tis far too risky."

"All the more reason to get the wedding we planned up and running and completed." Morgan made her way to Arlen's side.

Sean noticed she didn't contradict him, simply took the conversation in a different direction. He nodded to himself. Morgan was smooth like that. He was certain if he scratched the surface, she'd seeded her request with compulsion.

Arlen still looked as if he'd taken a mouthful of cod liver oil and was trying not to choke on it. "I'd planned on using this room," he aimed his words at Sean, "but—"

"All these old castles have chapels," Sean cut in.

"I've done everything I can to cleanse it of traditional religious taint. No crosses. No icons. I even painted Druidic runes on the walls. It might be perfect."

Gloria rubbed her hands together. "Splendid. We'll add a pentacle or two for effect."

"Excellent. Follow me." Sean started out of the great room that was still repairing itself. Getting away from the residual stench was a secondary perk.

"But don't I have to get dressed?" Katerina asked from somewhere behind him.

"Not important, dear," Liliana replied, her tone warm, reassuring. "You can always have a second, symbolic wedding later if you want a long dress and all the trappings."

"I suppose you're right, Mom."

"At least I have our rings," Arlen said.

"How?" Kat asked. "They were at our place."

"How else? I teleported home and retrieved them while you and your mum were talking."

Liliana caught up with Sean. "Is there anything I can do to help? I was cleaning up, and I'd almost finished dressing when I intercepted Mother's 'come right away' call."

"Aye. I got one of those from Arlen."

"At least you had your shoes on."

He glanced down and saw bare feet peeking out from under the hem of a long, colorful skirt. He remembered his sister wearing that same skirt a hundred years before. "Do you want to run upstairs and get your shoes?"

She shook her head. "I'm fine. Witches actually do best when there aren't so many layers betwixt us and the earth."

"Same holds true for Druids, and all other mages who rely on White Magic." Deeply pleased she'd sought him out, he reached for her hand, and she threaded her fingers in with his. It felt right to hold her hand, not awkward or unnatural.

"Anyway, is there anything I can do? You and Arlen and Gloria have the ceremony well in hand. Morgan too."

"Just be there for your daughter." Arlen hesitated and switched to telepathy. *"She's still running on overload. Your familiars are beautiful, stunning, but I saw Katerina's eyes when those birds flew downstairs, and she put two and two together."*

"She's wondering what other rabbits will jump out of the hat," Liliana agreed. *"She asked as much."*

"Do you think she believed you when you answered her?"

"Who knows?" An uncomfortable look washed over Liliana's starkly beautiful features. *"That's the problem with lying to someone. It's like an overdrawn bank account. Even if you never lie to them again, it*

takes time for them to come to trust what comes out of your mouth."

"*What are the odds of her getting her own familiar?*" He guided them up half a flight of stairs at the end of the hall. It led right to the chapel.

"*I have no idea. She might be too old. She might have come to magic too late. Or none of those things will matter at all.*"

"*Are the chances better once we leave modern time? And would a familiar confer added protections against Rhea and her ilk?*"

Liliana walked past him, through the stained-glass door he held open. "I have no idea," she said out loud. "Those are probably questions for Mom."

"Whatever it is, it will have to keep until later," Gloria said from behind them.

Once everyone had crowded into the relatively small space, she went on. "Take your places everyone. Open your hearts and your love. My granddaughter and her intended welcome you as guests at their nuptials."

Liliana untwined her fingers from his. Bending close, she whispered, "I'll be walking her down the aisle. Save me a spot next to you."

He'd have engaged in mortal combat with anyone who tried to get between them, but it wasn't an appropriate comment, not at a wedding. He smiled and said, "Always."

She grinned back. "I like the sound of that."

He did too. The funny thing was he meant it. He, who'd always steered clear of anything smacking of commitments beyond his financial responsibilities to his Druid clan.

"Mom. We're ready." Kat waved in Liliana's direction.

Will and Krista took up spots toward the front of the chapel and lifted flutes to their mouths. The high, sweet melody filled Sean's heart and soul with hope, partially scrubbing memories of the demon who'd penetrated his borders.

When the flutes began playing Mendelssohn's "Wedding March," Liliana and Kat wrapped their arms around each other's waists and walked the length of the transept to where Arlen waited. Gloria and Morgan bowed, greeting the couple-to-be and inviting everyone assembled to share their joy.

As the ceremony they'd hammered out unfolded, Sean felt proud—of all of them. If they were moving toward an all-out confrontation with evil—and it appeared they were—they'd need all the allies they could pick up along the way. That witches and Druids could find common ground was an auspicious beginning, indeed.

Liliana made her way to where he stood. He took her hand again. Together they let the magic of love and weddings and forever commitments wash over them. Afterward would be plenty soon enough to deal with the wreckage littering his great room and to craft a firm plan for their trip into time's vortex.

CHAPTER 9

*L*iliana had promised herself she wouldn't cry, but when Katerina pledged herself to Arlen, the tears she'd vowed not to shed welled anyway. Sean's fingers tightened around hers, and she squeezed back. Will and Krista's flutes soared to life playing Pachelbel's "Canon in D," and Arlen and Kat walked hand in hand from the chapel.

"Food and spirits are laid out in the kitchen," Morgan called after them.

Kat glanced back over a shoulder. "Maybe later. Arlen's all the food I'm interested in just now."

"I meant for after." Morgan's stern expression faded, replaced by a soft, wistful look.

Ribald suggestions rose from the group, along with laughter.

Liliana chuckled. "Why do I feel like I've been

transported back to a time when knights were bold, and ladies not nearly as prudish as the history books suggest?"

Sean smiled at her. It lightened his face and made him look like a mischievous youth. "Helpful commentary on bedroom practices is traditional, but I didn't think you were old enough to remember how everyone's relatives would stand outside the marriage bower trying to outdo themselves with smutty recommendations."

"Um, yeah. That practice had pretty much fallen out of fashion by the time I came along."

Gloria walked up to them, her blue-green eyes sparkling with satisfaction. "I thought that came off splendidly."

"It did," Liliana agreed. "Lovely job of taking the best from our handfasting tradition and blending it with Druid rites."

"It was seamless," Sean said. "When we were cutting and pasting sections, I had no idea it would play so well."

"Perhaps we'll start a new tradition," Gloria replied, "but for now we have a mess to take care of."

Liliana's chuckles morphed into laughter.

"I fail to see what's so funny." Gloria stared hard at her daughter.

"Nothing. I was just remembering how neat you like things."

Gloria made a noise between a snort and a grunt. "I swear, inculcating basic techniques for maintaining order—"

Liliana made a chopping motion. "Stop right there, Mom. I've managed. My house is put away enough I know where things are. It's what matters."

"I understand why the newly wedded couple won't be meeting us for toasts and food right away," Morgan said, joining them, "but I fully expect the three of you in the kitchen."

Liliana angled a glance at the Druid. "You have more than eating in mind."

"You bet, I do. We're running out of time. The marriage was a necessity, as is consummating it so it can provide the protections it was designed for, but the rest of us have to map out a firm game plan." Morgan paused for a beat. "When Arlen and Katerina are, uh, finished, we'll be gone from here."

"What do you mean running out of time?" Sean's pleasant expression turned somber. "Did you see something to alert you?"

She skewered him with her dark gaze. "You're the seer. Take a look for yourself."

"Maybe I will," he murmured.

Gloria motioned everyone toward the door. "We'll

join you in the kitchen after a quick stop to scatter sufficient magic around the great room to cleanse it of residual taint."

"See you soon," Morgan replied and exited the chapel, along with Will, Krista, and a few other Druids.

Liliana, Sean, and Gloria were the last ones in the chapel, and they hurried down the half flight of stairs leading to the main hallway. A faint touch of the demon's stench remained. Liliana set her teeth together with a *clack*.

Their respite was over.

Only problem was a face-to-face confrontation with Rhea Roskelly did more than scare her. It melted her bones to a puddle of terror so pervasive she wasn't certain she could go through with her part—whatever it ended up being. She still remembered Gloria hustling both of them to the cave where Rhea had launched unspeakable dark power. An unbreakable spell designed to ensure Katerina wouldn't escape her clutches like the last two potential Black Witches had.

If they'd been only a few minutes later, the die would have been cast, and Rhea would have claimed her daughter, much as she'd claimed Warren. Breath hissed from between her clenched teeth. After that incident, Liliana had restructured her life and created an impregnable fortress consisting of three elements.

Keeping wards around her daughter was her priority. Beyond that, she went to work and built impenetrable walls to ensure her nonexistent personal life remained that way.

No one expected doctors to be warm and fuzzy, so her med school credentials had opened the perfect door for her. Long before Kat's birth, she'd balked at actually attending formalized training, followed by a residency, but in the end it was easier than faking her credentials. She hadn't wanted any repercussions if someone examined her qualifications too closely.

The hard truth was she'd spent the last quarter century avoiding scrutiny and casting the occasional "don't look here" spell if the need arose.

If no one got close to her, no one else would be broken by her rampaging Black Witch kinswomen. The strategy had worked in her favor—for years. But it was about to change.

No, she corrected herself. *It's changed already.*

Gloria stopped at the entrance to the great room. "You two run along. That way I won't have to be particularly careful where my magic lands."

"Are you sure?" Liliana asked, not wanting to stick her mother with all the cleanup.

"Of course I am, or I wouldn't have offered. My bird and I can take care of this." She trotted nimbly forward, power sheeting from her. The raven shot forward, light flowing from it as it winged its way around the room herding and concentrating Gloria's magic.

"I'm impressed. Quite a useful assistant." Sean tucked a hand beneath Liliana's elbow and guided her away from the psychedelic lightshow turning the great room into a kaleidoscope of shifting forms and colors. The clean smell of witch magic, rich with vanilla and herbs, displaced lingering demon reek.

"Familiars are incredible. I was shocked—and delighted—when mine reappeared."

"Had it been gone, then?"

Liliana nodded. "For years. I shut the door on it after Warren's death, along with anything else that smacked of witchcraft."

"But you used your power in your work." His pace had slowed until they weren't moving at all.

She offered a wry expression. "I did, convincing myself all the while it had nothing to do with witchy anything."

He stepped so he faced her, a thoughtful expression creasing his forehead into a map of converging lines. "It must be difficult, having magic—powerful magic—that has the potential to turn wicked."

"You have no idea. When Mother said we had to tap into the teensiest corner of black power to make certain Rhea couldn't get to Katerina again, I was horrified. I only agreed because saving my daughter rose to the top of the heap."

"What aren't you saying?" His brown eyes never left her face.

"That I was terrified I'd turn to darkness, that I wouldn't be strong enough to resist the pull."

"It appears you managed." A corner of his mouth twisted downward.

"Thanks. It's been nearly thirty years, but not a day goes by that I don't do a reality check. Make certain I haven't slithered toward the abyss."

He dropped his hands onto her shoulders. Heat from his palms seared her, made her wish they could slip away and block out the world. "You've worried about something that will never happen."

She tilted her head, regarding him. "What do you mean? Evil is sneaky, seductive."

"Aye. 'Tis all those things and more, but it also requires willing participants. The reason Rhea got as far as she did with Katerina in that long-ago attempt to shanghai her loyalties—and her power—was because the child loved and trusted her great-great grandmother."

The truth in his observation kindled righteous anger, not just at Rhea but at herself for not taking a firmer stand. Rhea had done a number on Kat, who adored her. The child's face lit with pleasure whenever the old woman showed up. Made it damned difficult to bar the doors to her.

"Katerina did love Rhea—and it complicated everything. I should have banned her from the house. As it was, I never let her stay long, but I suspected she visited Kat's dreams. And snuck in at other times as well."

"Did you ask your daughter?"

"Yup. She always said no, but Rhea could have scripted that. Damn." She exhaled shakily. "I was such a fool, but Kat was too young for one of those heart-to-heart talks where you rip a child's innocence into bloody shreds by revealing someone they love is a monster."

"'Tis only in recent years we've treated children such. Back when I was born, they were dealt with like adults from the time they could perform useful chores."

She looked for censure in his words but didn't find any. He was merely stating a fact. Before she could respond, he went on, having switched to Gaelic. "Ye canna go back. And the net effect of what ye did—and dinna—do worked out."

"It may have." She lowered her voice. "But I'm scared. More than scared. I'm petrified. I'll face a million Father Abernathys before I'd willingly face

Rhea. The woman always terrified me, even as a child. I never could figure out why Katerina was so drawn to her."

He moved one hand from her shoulder to cup the side of her face. "Ye know the answer to that last part. Rhea is far from stupid. She made mistakes with you and your mum. Serious ones. By the time your daughter was born, she understood she was moving into her latter days, that she wouldn't get too many more chances to recruit another Roskelly witch."

"So she turned soft and fuzzy with Kat—after she murdered her father." The anger that had ignited burned with a steady flame. "I get what you said about today's children being overprotected, but I didn't have it in me to tell my daughter I'd lied about her father's death. Or that Rhea had killed him. For all I knew, she'd planted some kind of trap that would have sprung shut in Kat's mind if I'd told her everything."

She took a ragged breath. "I kicked it around with Mom, asked if there was some casting where we could test if Rhea had introduced things that shouldn't be there, but she said there wasn't. Not without endangering Kat's mind."

"I ken well enough. There are reasons aplenty Druids have never worked together with witches. We were never certain which ones were truly White Magicians and who was pretending."

She considered his words. "It's not just Druids and witches, though. Things may have changed, but the various types of magic-wielders have never trusted one another. Not enough to join forces."

"Ye'd be correct. Yet times are shifting, and our rift is coming to an end. Morgan invited me to cast my own vision of what we face. 'Twas a sound idea since we'll fare best if we have foreknowledge. Would ye do me the honor of joining me?"

A mountain of feeling swept through her. Pleasure at being invited. Dread of what she might view. Knowledge was a potent motivator, though. They'd prepare better if they had some idea what lay ahead.

"These visions"—she licked at dry lips—"how precise are they?"

"Verra precise, but ye must understand I see variations of possible futures. We willna know till we get there which one comes to pass."

Liliana leaned into the comfort of his hands before standing straight and rolling her shoulders back. "I'm game. We should stop by the kitchen and tell everyone what we're about. We can get something to eat and drink while we're there."

He nodded approval. "Ye may be scared, but ye're not letting it stop you. I respect that. I'm coming to care for you, Liliana."

Her heart skipped a beat or two before she

managed, "I like you too. A lot." She shut her mouth before she told him how she really felt. That looking at him heated her blood and made her long for the touch of his fingers and lips, for the surge of his cock inside her.

He angled his head and kissed her. Once she was surrounded by his scent, his taste, the desire she'd felt earlier swelled, turning her knees weak and slicking her thighs with need. Like before, the kiss didn't last nearly long enough.

He lifted his mouth from hers. "Sweet. So sweet." Threading an arm around her shoulders, he guided her toward the kitchen.

"Will we ever get a chance to...?" She didn't finish the sentence because all the words that danced through her mind made her sound like a sex-starved slut.

"I hope so, lass."

They shouldered through the swinging doors into the large kitchen area.

"There you are," Will cried.

"We were about to hunt you down with magic." Krista smiled and drained the wine glass in her hand.

"We shan't be here long," Sean said, switching back to English. "Morgan challenged me to scry the future. It's a damned good idea, so we're going to grab a couple of plates and maybe a bottle of spirits."

"Will you be in the basement?" Morgan asked.

"Aye. Where else? Our power is augmented by earth, and the subterranean aspect will make it easier for me. Plus, 'tis where all my accoutrements reside."

"All done." Gloria pushed into the kitchen, dusting her hands together. The raven flew ahead of her. With a delighted caw, it divebombed a plate of chicken and perched on a chair with a substantial chunk held in its beak.

Liliana had been piling food on plates. She edged toward the door with her bounty and silverware. Sean joined her with an open bottle of whiskey.

"Where are you going?" Gloria asked.

"With Sean to take a peek into the future."

Gloria furled her red brows. "Your owl will love it. They're natural seers, being Athena's bird and all. Remember? She was the goddess of knowledge, wisdom, and—"

Before her mother could wax prophetic about mythology, Liliana scooted through the door with Sean right behind her. "Which way?" she asked.

"To the right. Then take the second set of stairs that goes down."

She walked through another hall, an unfamiliar one. "How big is this place, anyway?"

He shrugged. "Something like a thousand square meters."

She did a few quick calculations and came up with

10,000 square feet. "Damn. I bet there are sections you don't visit for years."

"You'd be right about that." He grinned. "Take those stairs."

A blast of magic skittered around her, and a set of sconces flickered to life. Set into stone walls, they lit the way down a winding, wrought-iron staircase. Her owl stirred, very near the surface. She released it, and it flew ahead, candlelight glimmering off its golden feathers.

"That is one handsome bird," Sean said.

"Thank you. All magical birds are beautiful, but I fell in love with mine when it first showed up."

"How does the process work? Or is it something you can't talk about?"

They reached the bottom of the stairs. More candles shielded within glass lanterns burst into flame. "I suppose it's all right to tell you—since we're on the same side now."

"We always were. Druids were too stiff-necked to admit it."

"Witches too. Safety in insularity, eh?"

"Something like that. In here."

A door to her right creaked open, and she walked into a circular chamber with earthen walls and no windows. The hearth at the end held a floor-to-ceiling fireplace created of uneven river rocks. Like the candle lanterns, it too ignited, wood crackling in tune to Sean's power. Now that he wasn't shielding it, it flowed from him in sheaves of glorious light.

"How can you hold so much inside?" she asked, awed by how strong his magic was.

"Same way you do," he countered and set down the bottle of whiskey.

The owl swooshed past them, screeching its delight at being free. One more hoot was followed by it lunging into a shadowy corner. When it rose into the air again, a mouse squirmed in its hooked beak.

Liliana started to protest that her magic was nothing like his, but her words died unspoken. Because she'd opted not to use her power, she'd chosen to underestimate it. Acknowledging its breadth and depth would have meant she'd have to uncloak her ability—something she hadn't been willing to do.

Sean didn't say anything, but he watched her so intently, she was certain he'd been inside her mind. She set the plates on a low table in front of the hearth. He walked to the food and picked up a roll stuffed with something, chewing and swallowing quickly.

"Hold onto the account of how witches find their familiars," he said. "I'd love to hear it, but I need to concentrate on why we're here."

Liliana nodded. She felt the pull of power pulsing

through the chamber. Its earth-and-stone walls stood ready, a crucible strengthening Sean's magic.

"The way this will work," he said, "is I'll fill the cistern next to the hearth with water. Then I'll beg the goddess's grace and wait to see what she shows us." He moved to a spigot she hadn't seen because it blended in with the walls. The splash of water filling a cream-colored ceramic basin mingled with the hiss and snap of the fire.

While the bowl was filling, he knelt in front of a small credenza and opened its drawers, withdrawing packets wrapped in creased leather. The owl settled near him, talons curved around the top of a chair. It hooted softly, the mouse long gone. Unlike many birds of prey, owls didn't play with their food. Once they caught something, they ate it without fanfare.

Sean pulled the knots from leather cords, and the packages fell open. He lifted a golden chain from one and hung it around his neck. A striking fire opal was suspended from its links. He plucked a matching ring from another packet, sliding it onto his index finger. A pile of shiny stones came last. He carried them to the pool, shut off the water, and held the stones in his hands for long moments before casting them onto a small square of tapestry in front of the basin. They spun and quivered, finally rolling to a stop.

The owl flew to her, talons digging in as it perched on her shoulder.

"Come close," he said without turning around. "Once this begins, I'll be deep in trance."

Liliana crossed the room, stopping once she stood next to him. He began to chant in a low, musical voice, an old version of Gaelic rolling from his tongue. She held herself still, not wanting to interrupt his concentration. Long moments passed before the water's surface developed a choppy aspect and then began to swirl clockwise.

The owl's hold on her tightened. Apparently, it sensed something.

Sean was still chanting, louder now, more insistent. She followed most of the Gaelic as he instructed the water to reveal their future. After a final swirl, its surface smoothed. She bent forward, determined not to miss anything since she had no idea how long whatever he summoned would remain visible.

A medieval city formed, complete with walls. Was it Glasgow? No. The layout wasn't right. Not Edinburgh, either. She shuffled what little she knew about Scotland's major cities through her mind and determined they hadn't left Inverness. Maybe medieval had been somewhat of a stretch. 1700s might be closer. Made sense since Rhea had been born near the front end of that century.

Empty cobblestone streets filled with noise. People. Carriages. Just another day in a busy city. The owl hooted. She turned to shush it, but it had fluffed its feathers around it in a defensive stance. After its long absence from her life, she didn't have the heart to do anything but love it.

Moments later, she felt what the bird had responded to. Apparently, Sean did as well since the timbre and cadence of his words changed, and he moved to an entirely different casting. One she wasn't familiar with.

A shadow fell over the scene spread across the cistern's surface. Small at first, it grew rapidly. Horses whinnied, rearing with fear. People scattered every which way, shrieking and making the sign against evil. The owl hooted again, louder this time. A winged figure closed fast. Liliana curled her hands into fists, waiting to see what they faced.

She'd expected Roskelly witches, but contrary to popular opinion, witches couldn't fly.

Unless they borrowed steeds from hell.

A dragonesque form, black with a huge wingspan and shiny, double rows of teeth flew a few feet above street level, its wingtips brushing the buildings on either side. Rhea sat astride it, the same savage smile Liliana knew all too well plastered in place. Behind her, three more witches flew on similar steeds. The only difference was color. One dragon was red and three black. Fire spewed from their mouths.

She glanced at Sean. Sweat had broken out on his face, despite the room being on the cool side. The fire's heat mostly went up the chimney.

The next part happened in slow motion but was over in the blink of an eye. Rhea slapped the side of the dragon's neck. It turned until it faced them, whirling silver eyes hypnotic as hell. The owl screeched a warning just before Sean pitched headfirst into the pool.

Liliana sprang forward and grabbed a handful of jacket, but it burst into flames, burning her hand. Still, she didn't let go. Smoke rose, choking her. The owl dove forward, skimming the water's surface with its wings as power spilled from it.

"*Cut his casting,*" the bird shrieked into her mind.

She didn't waste time asking how. She didn't know exactly what to do, but she'd figure it out. Reaching deep, she threw her magical center wide open, grateful to the point of tears it responded. Her right hand was useless. The fire that had no visible source was scouring flesh from bone. She built a wall between herself and the pain and let magic flow through her, instructing it to undo Sean's spell.

The owl pinned its wings behind it and dove into the pool.

"Noooo," Liliana shrieked. She'd just been reunited with her familiar. Losing it again would be unbearable.

It surfaced, a plug in its beak, and she understood. No water in the basin meant a natural end to magic careening through the room like a runaway arcade game. She still clutched Sean's jacket. For a brief, heart-stopping moment, she'd felt it slipping from her fingers. Not because she'd let go, but because Rhea was doing her damnedest to draw him back through time.

Having snared him once, she had the feel of his energy. It would make capturing him a second time much easier. Liliana kicked herself for not thinking about that before.

Water gurgled down the drain. When the basin had emptied by half, the horrific scene, witches atop dragons, vanished. She dragged Sean backward until they both tumbled onto the dirt floor. He rolled off her onto hands and knees, coughing and hacking.

"Christ. Daft of me not to ward myself better," he said once he was done coughing water out of his lungs. "That craven bitch. She nabbed me once. Dinna even break a sweat to repeat what worked for her before."

Liliana had curled to a sit, nursing her wounded hand. Despite showering it with magic, it hurt like hell. "Yeah. She doesn't fight fair. We should remember that."

Sean crawled to where she sat. The owl was back. Rather than adding to her pain with its talons, though, it had settled on the floor leaning into her and linking its restorative magic to hers.

"Och aye, just look at your puir, wee hand. Ye and your owl saved me, lass. I'm forever in your debt."

Liliana raised her head and gazed at him. Water ran down his hair and the front of his shirt. Four reddened claw marks scored one side of his face. "Shit. She almost had you."

"Tell me something I doona know." His nostrils flared. "She had hold of me through time. Ye and the owl kept me anchored in this room. Druid power helped too, since I constructed this cavern with my own blood."

"How could she use your own spell to trap you?"

"'Tis time's curse, lass. Once ye open a channel, it runs both ways. Give me your hand. Let me heal you."

She held it out, wincing at the movement. "I've been working on it with my own magic. The owl's been helping."

He didn't say anything, but she felt a jolt as he joined his power with hers. The charred places turned red and then pink as flesh reformed. The spots where bone had shown through vanished. Best of all, the pain receded. She sucked a deep, cleansing breath into her lungs, blew it out, and did it again.

"Better." He shook his head. "I have no idea what Rhea's feeding from, but she's growing stronger."

The terror Liliana had dodged earlier returned with a vengeance, and something with sharp claws worked its way up her spine. It was tough to talk around the dry place in her throat, but the words had to come out. "If we can barely prevail with several centuries between us, how the hell will we manage confronting her in her own time?"

A muscle danced beneath one of Sean's eyes. "We will because we have to. There will be no peace for any of us until she and her band of dead Roskellys are confined to Hell."

"But isn't that where she's borrowing demons and dragons from?"

"Aye, the upper regions. We'll see her locked behind the gates of the Ninth Circle."

Liliana knew she was supposed to believe in magic to strengthen the odds of it working, but she didn't hold an optimistic view of their chances. Even if they shot Rhea's dragon out from under her and wrapped her in chains, the other three witches wouldn't let her go without one hell of a fight.

Sean stumbled to his feet and then offered her a hand to draw her upright. The opal suspended from his neck glimmered in light from the fire. She focused on how it reflected colors in hundreds of prisms to steady herself.

The owl floated upward, taking its place on her shoulder. *"I might have an idea,"* it said. *"Let me work on it."*

Before she could question it, the place it lived in her mind blanked out, and she understood it had left. Not hovering on the sidelines like it often did when it wasn't visible, but truly gone.

Sean let go of her long enough to scoop up the array of shiny rocks he'd cast in front of the basin. Once he'd dropped them into a pocket, he took her hand and they left the room. Being in the hall had a cleansing effect. Maybe she was feeling so dispirited because a chunk of Rhea had glommed onto her too.

Made sense. If both she and her grandmother had hold of Sean, he would have functioned as a conduit. Plenty of opportunity for Rhea to sow seeds of doubt and despair.

"Are ye feeling better, lassie?"

"A little. Guess she got to me through you."

"Ye nailed it. She's one conniving bitch and wouldna miss an opportunity to damage you any way she could."

Liliana closed her teeth over her lower lip so hard she drew blood. Of all people, she understood justice wasn't an element in the Black Witch lexicon. An image of Rhea, long, dark hair flying, straddling Warren as she bled him of anything resembling humanity rose to the fore.

She shook a fist at the empty hallway, determined to avenge his death.

And even more determined her grandmother wouldn't cause harm to anyone else she loved. Not now. Not ever again.

Sean concealed his shock at how easy it had been for Rhea to reach through time. He'd been warded, but not comprehensively. He couldn't maintain a ward and have sufficient magic left over to cast his scrying spell through its shielding.

Footsteps—lots of them—pounded toward them. The hollow ring of boots on stone sounded ominous, but he was still rattled—and furious—at Rhea Roskelly. She must have set markers for his particular magical signature. It was the only explanation for how she'd been aware of his casting almost the moment he'd created it.

Normally, scrying spells were stealth operations. Invisible on the receiving end.

Arlen raced toward him and Liliana, with Gloria

and Kat right behind him. "What the bloody fucking hell?" he demanded as he skidded to a halt.

"We felt power explode down here." Gloria's lips were skinned back from her teeth, and she looked fierce.

The other Druids, Morgan in the lead, ran to them, their expressions ranging from worried to angry.

Sean hunted for an explanation that wouldn't take forever to explain. "Time's curse boomeranged on me. I opened a channel. Rhea glommed onto it and reached through."

"Goddamn it." Morgan punched the air with a clenched fist. "This is my fault. I suggested you scry our future. Rhea must have been lying in wait for you like a hell-spawned bat."

"It's no one's fault." Sean wove a protective arm around Liliana's shoulders. "If it hadn't been for Liliana and the owl, though, I wouldn't be standing here."

Gloria's eyes widened. "Solid work, daughter. I take it you're done downplaying your magic."

"Christ, Mother. Do you have to turn every single misfortune into a lecture?" Liliana bristled.

"It was a compliment." Gloria bristled right back.

"Yeah, right. Cloaked in a rebuke."

"Stop it, you two." Katerina stepped between them.

Liliana slid from beneath Sean's arm and hurried

back toward his subterranean workspace. When she returned, she had the bottle of whiskey and was drinking from it. He took it from her and swallowed enough to welcome the burn as it coated his throat.

"Upstairs, everyone," Arlen, clearly back in command mode, instructed.

Sean thought about retrieving their plates, but they weren't important. He trudged up the stairs, shuffling options as he went. They couldn't do nothing, but Liliana had made a valid point when she'd choked out her worries about how they'd hold their own against dragon-riding witches.

The other problem was none of them who'd lived through the 1700s could remain there long. Not with the earlier version of themselves present as well. It wasn't insurmountable, but they'd have to locate their earlier selves and send them into the future to maintain a psychic balance point.

He rounded the corner into the upstairs hall with Liliana next to him. She'd been silent after the carping match with her mother, but her mind was busy. Concern mixed with determination streamed from her in waves. He shared both those emotions. Whatever they did next, they had to get things right. Being trapped in the past was a definite possibility if Rhea or her sisters cut them off from their magic.

A faint buzzing reminded him of the opal

suspended from its golden chain and the one on his index finger. Grateful for the help they'd provided, he removed the magical accoutrements and tucked them into a pocket where they joined the collection of power-imbued stones. He'd come within a hairsbreadth of getting sucked through the vortex he'd opened in time. It didn't require much of an imagination—or any scrying talent at all—to deduce what would have happened to him if Rhea had been successful.

Aye, she'd have fed me to one of the dragons.

After she bled me of my magic.

Everyone was gathered in the great room, the mood decidedly north of somber. Sean didn't blame them. They hadn't been called upon to be warriors for the better part of two centuries. Most of them were content wielding their power as a sideline and spending most of their time engaged in other pursuits.

Like his cozy desk at the bank.

Would he ever sit there again, pouring over columns of numbers on an encrypted Excel spreadsheet?

He pushed the thought to a distant spot. Like the food plates abandoned below, whether he ever held court over Druid money again wasn't at stake here. Arlen motioned him forward, and he joined the Arch Druid facing the group. He'd known Arlen too long not to recognize he'd already developed a plan.

Sean girded himself. Generally, if he disagreed with Arlen he kept it to himself, but this wasn't a time for blanket agreements. Each Druid's power held subtle differences. Arlen was more of a big picture guy, whereas Sean focused on details. Much like his financial work, lack of attention to the fine print was often your undoing in magical matters as well.

And then, they had to consider witch magic. Of the three Roskellys, Gloria was the only one confident in her power. The familiars added yet one more unknown layer. Sean nodded at Arlen, determined to make certain their discussion dealt with as many wrinkles as they uncovered.

Going into the past unprepared was far worse than not going at all.

Arlen's shrewd dark eyes settled briefly on each of them before he began to speak. "The reason I ended up Arch Druid was I charged into the midst of problems and managed to come up victorious. Not quite sure how I finessed it, but my luck always held." He took a measured breath. "Every one of those challenges presented a single path—at least to my way of viewing it. By following it to its endpoint, Druids prevailed.

"I'm having hell's own time locating that path for us now." He shook his head until his unbound dark hair danced around him. "I've played every option I can think of through my mind, but I'll be damned if I can see through to the endgame for any of them. Something clouds my vision, and it's making me deucedly uncomfortable."

He tilted his chin in Katerina's direction. "At first I told myself it was because I'm newly wedded and worried about protecting my wife."

"That's not it." Sean saved Arlen the trouble of blundering through telling them he had no bloody idea what they should do next.

Surprise scored Arlen's features as he turned to Sean, his almost invisible second. "Do you know what is?"

Sean quirked one brow. "Many things. We're outmanned and outgunned. The only way we'll power our way through this is by stealth."

"As in?" Arlen made come-along motions.

"Not certain. I'm still puzzling through it. We have assets. Blended magic is one. The familiars are another. We also have liabilities. We can't share the same time period with the earlier versions of ourselves. We're also vulnerable, more so than we would be here. It wouldn't take much for Rhea to trap us in the past. Cut off from our own time, we'd eventually fade."

"Why?" Liliana asked. "If your doppelganger wasn't there—assuming he moved to another time period—wouldn't it fix the problem?"

"Not entirely," Gloria answered. "It would mean

we could remain longer, perhaps years, but you can't stay indefinitely, living through the same eras a second time. It violates some sort of supernatural law."

"If that's true, how'd you manage to relocate to the 1890s?" Liliana turned suspicious eyes on her mother.

"Smart witch." Gloria sent an approving glance in Liliana's direction. "Two ways." She extended a finger. "Number one was that the earlier version of me was delighted to jump forward in time." A second finger joined the first. "She and I traded places every few years. We remained in our rightful time periods long enough to settle the energy, and then traded back. It was never my intention to stay in Old Glasgow forever."

"It would have been nice if you'd let me know," Liliana mumbled. "The other one never said boo, either."

"Maybe not, but she watched over you from a distance. If you'd needed me, I'd have been informed right away. I checked in on the two of you while I was here. All appeared well. You were doing fine without me. Kat thought I was dead. She also had no idea she was a witch." Gloria shrugged. "None of this is especially relevant to our discussion."

Sean turned his hands palms up, holding them in front of him like a balance point. "Unless we secure help from someone extraordinarily powerful, which is unlikely—"

"Like whom?" Arlen broke in.

"Oh, a god or goddess or someone like that," Sean replied.

"They've never bothered themselves with our battles," Arlen said crisply.

"Which is why I labeled it unlikely." Sean resisted a temptation to tell Arlen to shut up until he was done talking. "What's needed here is a sneaky, airtight plan. Something that has a high probability of success. Something Rhea won't recognize as a trap until the jaws have snapped shut."

Katerina straightened from where she'd been leaning against a wall. "I've said this before. I'm the logical bait. Rhea wants me, and she wants me badly enough to venture into our time to snag me. Years ago, she forged a link with me. I can't feel it, but I'm certain it's still there."

"Nay!" Arlen thundered. "I'll not risk you."

Katerina placed her hands on her hips. "Fine. You come up with a better proposal. Maybe if Mom and Gran can help me find my own familiar, I'll be stronger. Sufficiently resourceful to at least maintain Rhea in a holding pattern until the rest of you can capture her."

"We could try to lure a familiar." Gloria spoke thoughtfully. "Not normally how it's done, but—"

"I said nay," Arlen reiterated, but he wasn't shouting this time.

"If all fifteen of us travel backward in time," Sean said, "'twill create one hell of a psychic disturbance. Even the greenest magical neophyte would take notice of our arrival. That was one part of our plan that always bothered me. How we'd escape notice long enough to establish ourselves."

"Aye," Morgan broke in. "We canna turn around on tuppence. We have to show up, locate our doppelgangers, send them elsewhere..." She shrugged. "'Twon't happen quickly."

"And now that we know Rhea is on the lookout for us—or at least for Sean," Liliana added, "she'll be on us in a trice the second we break through anywhere near her time, wearing the same shit-eating grin she was sporting earlier."

Sean made a sour face. He'd noticed Rhea's expression—a cross between a starving piranha and a cagey hyena on the prowl. She'd looked at him as if he were a tasty treat, and he hadn't liked it much. If he hadn't been fighting for his life, her demeanor would have creeped him out.

Kat walked to Arlen and placed a hand on his arm.

"The whole reason we got married was to give both of us protections from my kinfolk."

"I haven't forgotten," he said gruffly. "'Tis hard to quantify such things. The marriage bonds are a hedge, but will they be enough? We've done a whole lot to anger Rhea. She's furious, and she's tapping into something to make her stronger than—"

"Because she feels cheated." Kat cut in without letting him finish. "If I were in her position, I'd be embittered too. In her world, being a Roskelly witch is the highest honor imaginable. To have first Gran and then Mom spit in her face must have infuriated her. And then, when she made a play for me, the child she groomed from infancy to love her, and I told her to go fuck herself..."

Kat shook her head. "If she weren't such a self-serving bitch, I'd feel sorry for her."

Liliana crossed to where Kat stood and hugged her. When she let go, she said, "I believe you're onto something."

"How so?" Kat asked.

"One of the first lessons in working with anyone is putting yourself in their place, understanding their mindset." Liliana paused to take a measured breath. "Everyone has a weak spot. Rhea's could be our rejection. If she's still raw and wounded, she just might believe you if you call her with magic and tell her you've had a change of heart."

"I'm not in favor of—" Arlen began.

Liliana kept on talking. "Lots of effective angles here. You could complain Mom and I kept you in the dark regarding your witch heritage. I don't have all the details about her dragging you backward in time from the Cameron crypt behind Inverlochy Castle's ruins, but you wouldn't be lying if you said you reacted badly because you were shocked by her revelation you were a witch."

Katerina nodded. "Yes. And now I've had time to think about it, to experiment with my power, I want more of it. Black magic will provide what's missing. Hell, if I take full advantage of it, I could displace every other cultural anthropology researcher, become the preeminent academic in my field."

"Perfect." Liliana tilted her head to one side, regarding her daughter. "I believe you could pull it off."

"And if she can't?" Arlen's tone could have etched glass.

Liliana leveled a pointed glance his way. "Well then, you and I will be engaged in a pitched battle to save her."

"Along with me and Sean and everyone else here," Gloria spoke up.

Sean waited. Would Arlen agree? If he didn't, they

could still proceed, but it would be awkward. He tried out—and discarded—things he might say. Arlen didn't require prodding, though. And he was so edgy, he'd resent almost anything that emerged from Sean's mouth.

Liliana's head snapped up. A smile illuminated her face, and the haunted look in her eyes receded. Witch magic crackled and sparked, turning the far side of the room incandescent.

The owl shot through a cloud of glimmering mist. Liliana ran toward it, catching it in her arms and transferring it to a shoulder. Sean expected the magical cloud to dissipate, but instead it thickened. The scents of leather and candlewax filled the room.

"Katerina." Liliana summoned her daughter.

Perhaps responding to the heady magic filling the room, Kat trotted lightly to her mother's side without asking a single question. Gloria joined them, an expectant expression illuminating her ageless face.

"How did you—?" she began, but Liliana waved her to silence.

Sean moved closer. Something momentous was unfolding, something ethereal. He sensed it, every magical antenna quivering with anticipation.

"Katerina Roskelly, daughter of witches," Liliana intoned in Gaelic. "Ye are but recently come into your magic, but a familiar seeks you. Do ye accept the bond with a pure heart and of your own free will? Acceptance means ye will value and nurture the familiar offering itself to you for the remainder of your life. No excuses. No regrets. 'Tis a lifetime commitment."

"I understand." Kat's voice trembled, but wonder shone from her eyes. "And I accept."

Amid a whooshing rush of air, the mist parted a second time. A mottled, dark brown eagle blasted through. Wings flapping furiously, it flew around Katerina's head as if taking her measure.

She held out her arm, and the bird settled onto it. Woman and bird regarded one another. Magic thickened and flowed between them, forming the same streamers Sean had seen connecting the other Roskelly women with their familiars.

Emotion thickened his throat. The bird was beautiful, magnificent. He'd wondered about the ceremonial aspect, and it had just unfolded before his eyes. Had Liliana sent her owl in search of a familiar for her daughter? It seemed likely.

Arlen made his way to his wife and her eagle. He bowed before the bird, addressing it in Gaelic. "'Tis an honor ye've bestowed on my mate. We both thank you."

The eagle cawed, hooted, and cawed once again.

The corners of Arlen's mouth twitched. "So that's

how it is, eh?"

More cawing followed.

Sean smiled, wondering what the bird had said. Arlen wrapped Kat's hand in his. "Your proposal is sound, darling. It's the most logical path forward, and I offer my support."

Sean blew out a tight breath. Even if it likely came at the eagle's behest, Arlen's acquiescence meant a lot. Their energies wouldn't be split. Such a simple thing might make all the difference. He started to ask about timing and where Katerina would go to maximize her attempt to summon Rhea.

Arlen saved him the trouble. "Today is mostly done," he said, addressing everyone in the room. "Eat and rest. Tomorrow near sundown, we'll travel to Inverlochy Castle. The Cameron crypt drew Rhea before, so 'tis the likeliest spot for Katerina to split the veils of time and talk with her kinswoman."

"I will tell her I've missed her," Katerina said. "Up until she tried to force me to her will, it was true enough. I will invite her to demonstrate her goodwill toward me by meeting with me in my own time."

"Non-negotiable," Gloria put in. "It might work. She'll respect you more if you come from a place of strength."

The eagle squawked, ruffling its feathers.

"So something like saying that this is my first, last, and only offer?" Kat furled her brows.

"Aye," Arlen replied. "Under no circumstance will ye retreat to the 1700s to parlay with her."

"No worries on that front." Kat thinned her mouth into a firm line. "Been there. Done that. Twice. Didn't like it much."

"We're agreed." Arm in arm with his wife, eagle still riding on her shoulder, they walked slowly from the room.

The magical nimbus the birds had emerged from was fading, leaving sparkly air and the faint scents of candle wax and oiled leather. Sean made his way to Liliana and her owl.

"I still want to know how you finessed that." Gloria looked askance at her daughter.

The owl hooted, fluffing its feathers. *"Not her. Me."* Its telepathic communication, pride laced into its words, was so clear, Sean heard it.

"You've done a most exceptional day's work," Liliana murmured and stroked the owl's golden-hued plumage.

"It truly has," Gloria said. "It simplified the process, and more importantly, cut the time factor."

"How does a witch normally find her familiar?" Sean asked, curious as always about how magical things worked.

"It takes weeks." Liliana still stroked the owl. "We fast and pray and enter trance states where we shroud ourselves in magic while remaining open to spirits flitting around us. I can't speak to how it is for other witches, but when the owl found me, I knew it was mine."

"I was there the entire time," Gloria said. "I formalized their bond with the ceremonial words that just passed between Lil and Kat."

"So it requires at least two of you?" Sean clarified.

"When there were more of us, the whole community of witches was involved," Gloria said. "A White Witch bonding with her familiar is a rite of passage, part of her journey to fully embrace her magic."

The owl hooted sagely, perhaps in agreement with Gloria's description.

"I make a point not to get too far ahead of the curve," Gloria went on, "but we've had a few key items go our way." She clicked them off on her fingers. "Kat and Arlen are married. Arlen's on board with Kat's plan to lure Rhea. Kat has her own familiar."

Sean nodded, hoping the items Gloria had mentioned would be sufficient. The slimy, nasty feel of Rhea's magic lingered, and his face still burned from where she'd branded him with her broken, filthy fingernails.

Liliana tapped her mother's shoulder. "You missed something."

"I don't think I did, dear."

"I've finally fully accepted my power. Surely it counts for something."

Sean looked from one Roskelly to the other, waiting. He'd done a lot of that today, but sometimes it was better than leaping forward and stuffing both feet into his mouth.

Gloria's imposing expression softened, and she replied in Gaelic. "Aye, daughter. It counts for more than ye'll ever know."

Liliana clearly hadn't expected her mother's answer. Her eyes sheened with tears. "Thanks."

"No need to thank me for speaking the truth." Gloria's tone was crisp. Turning, she walked briskly from the room.

Liliana turned to Sean. "Those abrasions on your cheek aren't looking all that swift. Come with me so I can clean them up."

He started to protest he could heal his wounds with magic, but he liked the thought of her touching him, fussing over him. Liked it enough to follow her as she hurried toward the archway at the end of the room.

The owl left her shoulder and flew in circles around them, hooting softly before it vanished. "Where does it go?" he asked.

"The familiars have their own place, not on Earth, but their own world. The owl accomplished a miracle today coming up with Kat's eagle. My guess is it's resting up, conserving its magic for tomorrow."

"I'm sorry it left so soon. I was planning to offer it carte blanche in the kitchen. Anything it wanted."

"I'm sure it'll take a raincheck on that." Liliana smiled and turned on the light in the first bathroom they came to. After flipping the hot water tap, she drew a washcloth from the rack and a scented soap ball from a dish on the tiled ledge.

Once she had a soapy mix in the cloth, she washed the wounded place on his face. "There," she said. "Now bend over the sink and rinse it."

He complied. "Why not simply use magic?" he asked.

"That comes next," she said and laid her fingertips on the hurt place.

A jolt of power rocked him, followed by intense heat that began in his belly and radiated to every cell in his body. He opened all his senses, human and Druid, desperately aware of Liliana standing inches away from him. Her scent. Her curves. Her sheer femaleness stole his breath.

Her green eyes had darkened to a mossy shade. Her mouth curved into a soft smile. "I'd take my time, be more elegant if we weren't heading into a full-blown confrontation with my witch ancestors tomorrow." She ran her tongue over her full lips. "My bird approves of you. It wasn't exactly a gamechanger for me, but it helps to have my familiar's blessing."

He gazed at her, drinking her in. "Tell your owl I appreciate its vote of confidence. Beyond that, what are you saying, lass?" He thought he knew, but he didn't want to mistake her intent.

"If you'll have me, I'd like for us to..." Color spread from her neck over her face, and she looked down for a moment, long lashes brushing her cheeks.

Sean had never felt more alive, more present. "I'm honored, and I'd like nothing better, but I have a condition."

"Only one?" She arched a dark brow.

"Aye, only one. Will ye join your life with mine. Not just in my bed right now, but forever more?" The words hurtled from a primal part of him. They shocked him yet felt right in a way very little else had for a long time.

She favored him with a smile worthy of Aphrodite and answered in Gaelic. "If 'tis the only way I can get ye out of those clothes, of course."

He scooped her into his arms and crushed his mouth atop hers. They had all night. This time, he wouldn't have to pull his mouth from hers before he was ready. As she molded into his arms, all heat and curves and need, his cock rose, pressing into her belly.

He groaned, desire rising in waves. While he could still think, he swept an arm beneath her legs and carried her out of the bathroom and down the branching maze of hallways to his rooms.

CHAPTER 11

*L*iliana welcomed the press of Sean's lips, the surge of his tongue inside her mouth. She wrapped her arms around his neck about the time he gathered her into his arms and carried her out of the bathroom and down the warren of halls that bisected the castle, never breaking their kiss.

The owl had been full of surprises today. First, the eagle. She had no idea what inducements the owl had offered. Or perhaps merely putting out a distress call to other potential familiars had been adequately motivating. Once the bird was done preening and prancing on her shoulder, its parting shot had been to not let Sean get away.

All her years with Warren, the owl had been vocal about its disapproval. Even though Warren couldn't see her familiar, the bird had played tricks on him.

Moving items to a different spot or brushing a wingtip across his face. If Liliana chided it, the owl told her to fess up and tell her husband what she was.

She'd tried. Sought out opportunities, but how do you tell a human magic is real? Every time she'd started to stumble through an explanation, Warren had broken in, come up with a reason for why she'd slipped into Never Never Land. She was tired, overwrought. She'd be more balanced in the morning, or after she slept or ate something.

Gazing at the love and trust shining from his eyes, she'd never had the stomach to disclose that their entire life together was based on a lie. A damned big one.

Once he was dead—and she was wallowing in bitter guilt—it had been easy to build walls, ignoring her owl. Eventually, it gave up trying to reach her, but its absence added to her shame. The bond was forever.

She'd failed on yet one more front.

It didn't help when her mother peppered her with "I told you so" commentary. If she hadn't had raising her daughter as a focal point—and her job at the hospital—she might have lost it. No wonder she'd done everything in her power to shield Katerina from knowing anything about her witch heritage...

A door opened before them, and Sean carried her into a generous room lined with windows. A large bed covered with a quilted duvet cover and many pillows was tucked into one corner. A generous desk loaded with computer equipment into another. Stout carved wooden furniture was scattered about. Mostly dressers and shelves overflowing with books and scrolls. The overall impression was homey, but with a definite masculine flavor. Doors were cut into two walls, presumably one led to a bathroom.

She still had her arms twined around his shoulders, and her mouth glued to his. The air around them flared with magical energy, and his clean fresh scent, wet moorlands, heather, and gorse filled her nostrils.

She inhaled hungrily. A woman could live on that smell, absorb it into her pores. Into her soul. And keep returning to the well for more.

Sean broke their kiss and set her on her feet, his dark gaze boring into her. "Are ye certain of this, lass?"

Liliana nodded. He must have tapped into her roiling thoughts as he carried her the length of the castle. "More certain than I've been of anything for a long time. I attempted to build a life with someone who wasn't magical. I was foolish to try and too self-righteous to admit I was wrong—until it was too late."

"Can ye clear your mind of aught but us?"

"I already have." She pushed his sweater, a creamy-soft cashmere affair, off his shoulders and attacked the buttons holding his shirt together. The last one was tangled up in thread. In the end, she broke it and shoved the linen aside, running her fingertips across acres of muscled skin. Sean rolled his shoulders, and his shirt fell to the floor. His torso was sculpted, gorgeous. A study in Greek god perfection. Slabs of muscle wound down his upper arms. A dusting of dark hair ringed copper-gold nipples puckered with sexual heat.

He watched her intently, dark eyes burning with need. A quick flash of magic removed the long ivory tunic she'd layered over a colorful skirt. One minute, it swathed her. The next it joined his shirt on the floor. Liliana grinned. "Neat trick. You'll have to teach it to me."

"Trade secrets, lass." He grappled with the hooks holding her bra in place and tugged until it fell aside, freeing her breasts.

Suddenly shy, she looked away. No one had viewed her body in years. Would he find it pleasing? A strangled-sounding gasp rose from him just before he filled his hands with her breasts.

"Beautiful, lassie. So beautiful. Ye're like a goddess." He rubbed her stiff nipples between his fingers sending jolts of sensation cascading through her. She darted forward and licked one of his nipples. He made a decidedly male sound. She took it as encouragement and sucked on the bit of flesh until it hardened still more.

He was doing wicked things to her breasts with his fingers, and she leaned into his touch, savoring everything about being with a man again. Damn but she'd missed the warmth and intimacy, the shared confidences, the sense of having a special safe place with her closest friend. She'd missed sex too. The heat. The excitement. The barely being able to breathe sensation as need tightened her belly.

She lifted her head from swirling her tongue around his nipples. Bending forward, he crushed his lips atop hers again. She opened her mouth to his kiss, welcoming the thrust of his tongue as he explored. Arousal tingled and zapped, making her lightheaded as she kissed him back. His lips were full, firm, and insistent, asking for more.

Demanding everything she had to give.

She opened her heart and soul to him, holding nothing back.

He strung kisses over to her neck and ear before returning to her mouth, all the while teasing her nipples. She sucked his lower lip, ran her lips over his stubble-covered cheeks and chin before settling them on his again. Her legs felt shaky, arousal so thick she inhaled it with every breath. Where he rubbed them, her nipples swelled to greater fullness, and her breasts grew heavy with need.

He straightened, gazing at her as if she were every

wonderful gift he'd ever received rolled into one. Dropping his hands to her waist, he undid the fastenings holding her skirt in place. It had a complicated button closure pattern, but he didn't miss a beat. The garment slithered to her feet where it pooled in a heap of silk and organdy, an old-fashioned cotton fabric. She hadn't bothered with underwear, and her feet were bare, courtesy of her frantic dash downstairs after Gloria's summons.

So much had happened in such a short time, she felt caught up in a whirlwind of demon attacks, weddings, witch strikes, and now a surfeit of sensation courtesy of the Druid looking at her with fire burning in the depths of his eyes.

Fire that would sear her soul now that she'd dropped her barriers and let him in.

"Not fair," she managed. Every drop of moisture in her body had headed south, and her throat was so dry the sides rubbed together.

"What isna fair, lass? I'm gazing at the finest example of womanhood imaginable. And reveling in every minute."

She giggled. At least it brought a small bit of saliva back into her mouth. "You still have clothes on, and you're making me sound like a prize horse."

"Aye, they're beautiful too, but in a far different

way." A smile began in his eyes before it curved the corners of his lips.

She reached for his belt, unbuckling the smooth leather. Next, she undid the button and zipper holding his trousers in place. They glided down his slender hips and high, tight ass. He toed a shiny pair of loafers off and stepped out of his pants. The only thing left was his shorts.

Back to struggling for breath, she placed a hand over the tented-out front of his underwear. The ivory silk fabric was warm to the touch as she curved her fingers around his erection. Suddenly, she couldn't wait to see him, and she tucked her other hand into his waistband, dragging it downward. Once it cleared his cock, she untangled her other hand and pushed until his shorts were well on their way down his legs.

Almost reverently, she ran her fingers the length of his erection. Long, hard, hot, perfect, it sprang into her hand, begging for all the attention she could lave on it. He slid his hands beneath her hair, cupping her head between them. Slow, lazy, deliberate, he kissed her again. The kiss of a man claiming his woman, his intent unmistakable.

She still had a choice—if she'd wanted one, which she didn't—but it was vanishing fast. When she looked past her desire, her path was clear, uncomplicated. If she walked away from Sean, she'd regret it forever. Not a mistake she was willing to make.

He lifted his mouth from hers. "Look at me, lass."

She stared into the raging inferno of his eyes, cock still sandwiched between her hands. Her focus sharpened. Pieces of her life clicked into place, rearranging themselves to include him. When the dust cleared, he was a part of her, had always been a part of her, would be joined with her forever.

"Ye are blood of my blood and bone of my bone." His voice was so deep and rich, chills ran through Liliana. "Repeat after me, lass."

Once she did, he gripped her head more firmly, still gazing into her eyes. "I give you my body that we may be one. I give you my spirit till our life shall be done. Ye are blood of my blood and bone of my bone."

Liliana repeated the incantation, recognizing the Druid wedding ceremony from Kat and Arlen's joining.

Sean wrapped them in magic and toppled them onto the bed behind them. They floated downward, cushioned by power until the softness of the duvet met her bare skin. The hunger she'd felt before paled in the face of the full-on lust branding her, marking her as his. She twined her arms and legs around him, exploring his body with hers.

He kissed her, slow and deep, before drawing his

lips down her body, taking his time as he licked and suckled the hollow between her collarbones, her breasts, her stomach. Every spot where he touched her caught fire until she was amazed she didn't explode into a fiery ball that ignited everything it touched.

He pushed her legs apart and teased her nub with the very tip of his tongue. She screamed and made a grab for his head, forcing contact. He resisted, licking around her aching, throbbing clit. Around it. Up one side, down the other. A swirl across the tip.

She was panting, barely breathing, heart thumping so hard it was almost beating outside her body. In one fluid motion, he plunged two fingers inside her and fastened his mouth on her nub, sucking hard. The climax that had hovered, elusive, just out of reach, pounded through her.

Wave after wave of heat and sensation attacked her, crested, and then did it again. Somewhere in the midst of things, he shifted position, kneeling between her legs with his cock seated at the entrance to her vault. She lifted her hips and wrapped her legs around his waist, desperate for the hard length of him inside her.

His head was thrown back, neck corded with passion as he sank into her. She tightened herself around him, never wanting to let go. He felt incredible, filling her, plumbing her, loving her. Slowly, ever so slowly, he withdrew until just the tip of him teased her nerve-rich entrance. And then he sank back inside.

Pinned beneath him, she writhed, wanting him to move goddammit, to fuck her hard and fast and forever. She loved looking at him, at the play of muscles moving beneath skin, at the flex of arm and legs and torso as he made love to her. When he moved his head forward and opened his eyes, they were filled with tenderness and hunger and love.

The floodgates within her that had cracked open earlier responded. She spread her arms, and he lowered himself atop her, holding her close. Her breasts were crushed against his chest, and she tightened her legs around his back, rocking against him.

This time when he withdrew, he slid back inside sooner. His breath rasped, warm against her mouth, and he tasted sweet. Of futures and promises. She drenched them in magic, urging him to come, to consummate their spiritual union.

He drove into her, all restraint shattered. She rose and fell with him, straining for another release. Nothing gentle or civilized about their bodies crashing together. This was sex. Raw, primal, push-to-the-limits sex. The wave she was chasing thundered over her, and she shuddered around him. He ripped his mouth from hers, cried out, and his cock quivered with orgasm, shooting jets of semen into the deepest, most private part of her.

They clung to one another, grinding their bodies together until the spasms quieted. He smoothed hair away from her sweaty face and turned them onto their sides with his cock still buried in her body. "Thank ye, *léannan*. Darling."

She breathed him in, content in the circle of his arms. "I don't know who should be thanking whom, but that was unbelievably wonderful." She moved back enough to trace the line of his cheekbone with her fingertips.

"The Druid joining ceremony..." Liliana hesitated, not sure how to couch what she wanted to ask.

"Is actually borrowed from the Celtic gods, and 'tis just as significant when we utter the words ourselves," he replied, divining her question. "Like with your handfasting ceremony, 'tis a thing two people can do absent a third to officiate."

A smile danced around her lips. "So we're, um, married?"

"Not in the modern sense, where couples run for a divorce lawyer at the first sign of trouble. This is forever."

The words they'd shared rolled through her mind.

Blood of my blood and bone of my bone. I give you

my body that we may be one. I give you my spirit till our life shall be done.

"If the vows protect Arlen and Kat, then they should do the same for us," she ventured.

He nodded. "'Twas my hope, but not my main motivation." He tucked her head into the hollow between his neck and shoulder. "I don't fully understand how these things come to be. Why I've spent hundreds of years alone, but the moment I laid eyes on you, I knew you were different. That you were the woman I'd spent my life waiting for."

"Did you question the knowing?" Her words were muffled against his skin.

"Aye, lassie. But then I question everything." He'd lapsed back into Gaelic. "The important thing is I dinna question it for long, nor did I pick it apart until naught was left."

She chuckled. "Is this when we admit all our less than stellar traits? After the deed is done and we're stuck with one another?"

A deep, rumbly laugh, rather like a merry grizzly bear, filled her ears. "Now that ye mention it, what deep, dark secrets do ye harbor?"

"You already know all of them. I was ambivalent about witchcraft, about magic. I can be rash and headstrong." Her bantering tone dropped away. "And when I love, I love with a ferocity that knows no bounds. I would have done murder to keep my daughter safe from Rhea. Nothing has changed about that."

"It may come to that."

She scrunched her forehead into worried lines. "What do you mean? Rhea and her nefarious sisters are already dead. Killing them twice won't change anything."

"Dead is relative, lass." He was back to English. "The more I've thought about this, the more unlikely we are to have the luxury of escorting a hissing, spitting, screeching Rhea to the Ninth Circle of Hell."

"But I thought that was the whole purpose of tomorrow. I'm confused."

"Tomorrow's purpose is making certain Rhea isn't bouncing in and out of Kat's life—or yours—with unpleasant surprises. Like unsolicited trips to the past. If we behead her and burn her remains, it will be just as effective as sealing her behind the Ninth's Circle's gates."

"Are you certain?"

"Nay, but it's always prudent to have a backup plan. Rhea may heed Katerina's call, but when she shows up, she won't be alone. She's old and canny and has no reason to trust any of you. You've stabbed her in the back enough times, she'll be wary."

Liliana closed her teeth over her lower lip. "What

about those dragon things? Or the demon that was trying to batter its way into your castle?"

"If the question is whether she'll rustle up monsters and have them ride shotgun, I'd give it even odds."

"So we might face her, other Roskellys, and an array of Hell's denizens."

Sean nodded. "The other problem is Kat will initially be by herself. The rest of us will have to conceal our presence behind bombproof, invisible warding."

Alarm bells tolled in Liliana's mind. "But those take time to dismantle. If we have to move quickly—"

"Exactly. It might not be fast enough."

"Crap. I'm not sure I want Kat to risk herself. Too many unknowns."

"I don't see any good options. You could try to get Rhea's attention, but she'd see right through you. Same holds true in spades for that mother of yours. She's got magic to burn, and an attitude to match."

"You've got Mom's number." Liliana rolled her eyes. "She always was one tough broad, but her heart's been in the right place."

"Aye, and she'd move mountains to keep her family safe," he agreed and threaded his fingers through her hair. "No matter what befalls us tomorrow, I'm ever so grateful for you. For your beauty. For your love. For throwing your lot in with a poor sod like me."

"Poor sod, my ass. Aren't you the mastermind who keeps your cheerful band of Druids rolling in sanitized cash?"

"Ha! My one useful trait."

She tightened her body around his still-hard cock. "Oh, I can think of a few more that have nothing to do with spreadsheets."

He furled one dark brow and repositioned their bodies so she was on top, straddling him. "There are many kinds of sheets in the world, *mo léannan*. Shall we take advantage of the ones that lie beneath us?"

Part of her wanted to get tomorrow nailed down until no more unknowns existed, but it wasn't possible. He grasped her hips and rotated his cock, moving it from side to side.

An idea flirted with her but fled as soon as he took her breasts, one in each hand, rubbing her nipples to peaks. Desire rose, thick as clotted cream, wiping out everything but the man beneath her. Her heart, her life, the one she'd pledged herself to without hesitation or a backward thought.

She could chase the idea afterward. The one that had tantalized her with an elegantly simple solution, one that would keep Katerina, her Katerina, safe from harm.

Sean bent to lace knee-high soft leather boots. He adjusted the tartan wrapped around him—an old-fashioned style that swathed his torso too—and checked the items he'd added to a sporran. The opals matched to his magic adorned his neck and hand; additional stones rattled together at the bottom of the sporran. Ever since he'd awakened with Liliana sleeping next to him, he'd been split between making certain everyone had what they needed for tonight's confrontation and stopping to feast his gaze on her.

Everything she did intrigued him. He could have watched her forever and died content. Her movements were precise, graceful, with little wasted motion. A few moments ago, she'd braided her hair into many plaits and tied the lot of them together to keep everything out of her face.

"There you go again," she said from where she was pulling on a long black skirt she'd found in his clothing trunks. Her cloak, clean and dry, was draped over a chair.

"There I go again, what?"

She smiled indulgently. "Whenever I look up, you're watching me."

"I like looking at you, lass."

She buttoned the skirt into place and shook her head. "It runs deeper than that."

"Aye, that it does. I'm still marveling at having a mate after all these years."

"Any regrets?" It was her turn to rake him with her sharp, green eyes.

"Not a one. Yesterday was intense, but I'd make the same choices today. Or tomorrow."

Her smile widened. "Tell me again why you're dressed in ceremonial garb? I'm not complaining." She continued to regard him. "I don't know what it is about kilts, but they have more character than pants."

"'Tisn't just me. All of us selected clothing that won't stick out like a bloody enemy flag—just in case we end up at the wrong end of Rhea's vortex. In our case, the kilts don't signify clan affiliations. Scottish Druids never rolled that way, but those who've lived long enough all own tartans of one design or another."

Liliana pursed her mouth into an unreadable line and walked until she stood facing him. "I have an idea. It may not work, but it's been banging about in my head since we got up."

Her tone—deadly serious and edged with uncertainty—alerted him he might not like what she had to say. He stopped fiddling with the sporran. "Let's hear it."

"All right." She pinched her nose between her thumb and forefinger before looking squarely at him. "Something you said last night about having to shield ourselves, so Rhea and whoever she carts along with her won't know Kat's not alone, got me thinking."

Sean nodded encouragement. He remembered that part of their conversation quite clearly. It had occurred just before the second time they made love.

"Kat and I have a similar feel, energy-wise. I suspect it comes of both of us having human fathers."

Sean narrowed his eyes. He had a feeling what she'd say next, and she didn't disappoint him.

"I'm a little unclear on the magic that could finesse this, but what if I used a glamour? Made myself look like Katerina? I wouldn't be all that close to Rhea, and maybe—"

"Ye're joking."

"Nay, I'm not," she replied aping his Gaelic before continuing in English. "It's not all that farfetched. When I was much younger, many of the witches at gatherings wore glamours. No one wanted to be identified in 'real life' for what they were." She winced. "What I thought was they didn't trust Mom or me, being Roskellys and all. None of the others had our Black Magic blood."

He took a deep, steadying breath. He'd assumed Liliana would be by his side the whole time they were in Fort William.

By his side.

Not masquerading as a stand-in for her daughter.

"Have you discussed this with your familiar? Or anyone, for that matter?"

She shook her head. "Thought I'd start with you. So far, you haven't given me any solid reasons why it won't work."

He raked a hand through his hair. "Rhea Roskelly is your kinswoman. She's linked to you by blood, and she's known you all your life. The same holds true for Katerina. Do you honestly believe she won't notice right away that you've tricked her—or tried to?"

Liliana squared her shoulders. "Define right away."

"Och aye, lass. Perhaps in the first ten seconds. Thirty if she's a wee bit slow on the uptake." That he'd reverted to Gaelic told him he was upset. His first tongue was always his fallback when he didn't want to waste energy finding just the right nuance in English.

"I figured I might have a few minutes."

He opened his mouth, but she held up a hand. "Hear me out before you tell me I'm full of shit. Rhea is dead. It confers some advantages, but one of the big disadvantages is she can't think as clearly, probably because she's lost a number of brain cells to decomposition. She'll just have traveled through time, a disorienting process if my experience is any bellwether.

"Between those two, I thought I might fool her. Particularly if I start talking the second she stops shimmering between worlds. And if Kat and I trade familiars—"

"Is such a thing even possible?"

"I don't know. I was going to ask the owl—or Mother." She chewed her lower lip thoughtfully. "If I showed up with the eagle, it would throw Rhea off balance. She'd recognize my owl in a heartbeat, but she'll not have laid eyes on Kat's brand new familiar."

"Does she have a familiar of her own?" Sean asked.

"No. The animals are decent. They'd never link to anyone wielding dark power."

Sean huffed out a tense breath. When he looked for holes, weak places in her strategy, he couldn't find obvious ones. Anyone who served as their sacrificial sheep would be putting themselves at huge risk.

She nailed him with her direct gaze. "My plan isn't as bad as all that, is it?"

"Not if you can swap familiars," he agreed grudgingly. Making a fist, he punched the air. "Damn it, Liliana. I'd rather not do this at all. Take our chances Rhea won't bother us as much as she has been."

"Do you honestly believe she'll let us be?" She knitted her dark brows together. "Christ, Sean. She hates Druids the same way she hates anything that smacks of clean magic. Arlen's link with Kat has to have infuriated her, particularly since she wanted Kat for herself. She didn't know about you and me until she saw us together yesterday. I'm certain she's put two and two together by now."

Liliana stopped to take a breath. "I know that old woman. She's intransigent, and she won't stop until she's exacted the revenge she's certain she deserves. Retribution for breaking the long and illustrious line of Roskelly witches."

Sean wanted to deny the truth in her words, tell her she was overreacting, but he refused to lie to her. "Ask your owl if that part of your plan is possible."

Her expression softened. "Thank you."

"Ye needn't offer thanks—" he began.

She cut him off. "Look. I know you don't want me to risk myself. Hell, it's not my first choice, but neither can I stand by and watch my daughter do what scares the crap out of me." Liliana stood taller. "I did Kat a disservice when I shielded her from her heritage. If she'd grown up practicing magic, I wouldn't be so quick to jump in."

Worry for her ate at him like acid, but he couldn't sequester her in a tower. Rapunzel had gone out of fashion a few hundred years before. "Not that I don't have faith in you"—he was back to English—"but you haven't exactly put in the time honing your own ability," he pointed out.

"Maybe not, but I'm better than she is. Pfft. Mother's the one who could probably pull this off best, but she's magical through and through. Sorcerer father, Black Witch mother. Rhea would smell her out damned fast."

The air hummed and vibrated with the feel of witch power. Sean's head snapped around in time to see the owl fly through a rent in the ether, amber eyes glittering with anticipation. After a few circuits of his bedroom, it lit on the edge of his desk.

Liliana beckoned to it, but it remained where it was.

"You share my thoughts," she said, directing her words at her bird. "Is it possible for Katerina and me to trade familiars for a brief time?"

The owl fluffed its feathers. *"I can appear by her*

side, and the eagle by yours, but the magical connection will be absent."

Sean inclined his head. "Thank you for including me in your reply. Do you mean the streamers I've seen flowing between you and Liliana?"

The owl hooted. Sean took it as a yes.

"Rhea won't be focused on the fine points," he said, his words slow and deliberate.

"My take as well," Liliana agreed. "If you have what you need, let's run this by the others." She picked up her cloak and slung it around her shoulders.

"I don't suppose there's any way to talk you out of it."

Liliana shook her head. "How could I stand by and send my daughter—ill-prepared because of my fears for her—into an arena where she'll have need of the power she only recently discovered she has?"

Sean wrapped his arms around her and kissed her forehead. "I love you, Liliana, and I'll do everything in my power to keep you safe."

She reared back and met his gaze. "I know you will. Keeping all of us safe is high on my list too."

He remembered how she'd held onto him, fought for him when Rhea was intent on dragging him backward in time. "We'll get through this," he said, his voice rough with emotion.

"Of course we will. And once we have, I want to go away together just the two of us."

The owl squawked and flew to her shoulder, latching on. "You too," she told her familiar. "But then you don't require an invitation."

They hurried from his rooms, intent on locating the others.

An approving hoot warmed Sean. They had blended power on their side. He tried not to think about dragons and demons and other wicked hell-spawned monsters. They'd be in the thick of it soon enough. He'd fight what was in front of him. And he'd believe in his allies and their invincibility. To put a finer point on it, he believed in Druids and in Liliana. In her clean, pure power, and in her love for her daughter, a love that was driving her to put herself in the line of fire.

It was the way all battles were won. By holding faith in yourself and your cause as you meted out death one enemy at a time.

It was long past an early dusk when their convoy of three cars pulled up in a vacant church parking lot a few city blocks from Inverlochy Castle in Fort William. The sky was thick with clouds, but it wasn't raining or snowing. Not yet, anyway. They'd agreed on the church as a staging area since its religious atmosphere and collection of icons would mask their presence as well as anything. Rhea might have spies in modern time, a distinct possibility since she'd known exactly when to snatch Katerina a few weeks before.

Kat had been vehemently opposed to her mother's proposal, but Arlen glommed onto it like a lifeline. No one knew better than him how magically inexperienced his wife was.

Except maybe Liliana. Between her and Gloria, they'd brought Kat around to Plan B.

As soon as Sean's car rolled to a halt Liliana jumped nimbly out, losing herself in a shadowed alcove of the sprawling church. When she emerged, his eyes widened. She could have been her daughter's twin.

Gloria regarded Liliana with a critical eye, walking all the way around her. At length, she nodded. "It just might work. If I don't dig too deep, you feel enough like Katerina to be credible."

"I'll make it work." Liliana's words held a fierce undertone. "It's that way. Right?" She pointed to the west.

"Aye." Sean fell into step next to her with Arlen and Katerina right behind them. They'd station themselves in a neighboring crypt, close enough for Liliana to have access to Kat's eagle. Hopefully their presence wouldn't be overly noticeable. The spirits of the dead would help with that. They'd compromised on the extent of their warding. It had to be sufficiently dense to partially mask their presence, but not so thick it would eat up precious minutes dismantling, if they needed to move fast.

The other Druids and Gloria would be on the castle grounds, concealed within Inverlochy's ruins. Because they were farther away, they wouldn't employ the bombproof warding that took forever to pull apart, either.

Sean reached for Liliana's hand. She laced cold fingers in with his. "I'll enter the crypt," she murmured. "Once I'm inside, I'll call Rhea."

"No magic," he cautioned.

"I understand." Her voice was subdued. "Absent magic, she might not hear me, but even if she does she'll be antsy as a scalded cat, alert for anything out of place."

"You may look like Kat," Arlen said from behind them, "but everyone's magic has its own unique feel."

Sean glanced over a shoulder at Arlen. "She knows that."

"Sorry. I was trying to be helpful."

"What happens if things go to hell?" Liliana asked.

"We'll be right there." Sean tried to infuse confidence into his words. They'd be there unless she was swept into a portal. Once that happened, they'd have to chase her energy to locate her. Possible, but not the easiest proposition.

"Aye, we're becoming seasoned veterans traveling through time," Arlen murmured.

"There's a flat place in the vortex between eras as the veils of time part to allow you through," Sean said. "'Twill be Rhea's casting, so she'll be helpless to alter the destination, but you can."

"How? Even in the safety of my own basement, I could barely manage to kindle a spell to take me through time."

"Remember the elements of that spell?" Sean asked. Once she nodded, he went on, "The spot where you add a location, concentrate on finding and altering it. You needn't make much of a change to come out in a different spot from her."

"Got it. Once I'm there, I put a reverse casting together?"

"Aye. You have the elements with you, right?"

Liliana nodded. "The herb packet is tied in a square of linen in a pocket. The timber shard from your castle too, and the vial of your blood."

"Ye gave her your blood?" Arlen's words were barely audible, but shock ran through them.

"Och, and I ken 'tis a risk. Still, 'tis also the most expedient way for her to find me and return home." He and Liliana had chosen not to mention their newly formed bond to the others because neither wanted to divert the group's attention from the task at hand. The bond made his blood an even greater gift. A drop or two sprinkled on her other ingredients should bring her right back to him—no matter where he was.

"The vial is masked with my magic," Liliana said.

"Let me take a shot at it." Kat's voice was strained. "At least it won't command Rhea's immediate attention if it feels like me."

Liliana turned and passed a small, stoppered cylinder to Katerina. Magic pulsed and flared before she handed it back.

A few more steps and they reached the car park for Inverlochy Castle. Because of the hour, it was empty. Liliana drew her cloak more firmly around her. The night was damp and cold, but she probably fought an inner chill as well. Her words clinched his impression.

"I'm scared, but my fear could work in my favor. No one summons a Roskelly witch lightly."

Sean would have traded his life to spare her what would unfold soon, but he'd never been into high drama. The only two realistic options were her or Kat, and he respected Liliana for stepping up to the plate. Some—or all—of them storming the past in search of Rhea and her sisters held far more danger.

"When you go into the crypt," Kat said in a low

voice, "walk to the end. You'll find another set of steps. Go down those to the lower level. It's where she nabbed me from."

"Thanks. I'd probably have stopped as soon as I entered the place. Those old gravesites give me the creeps." Liliana raised a hand. Power crackled from her fingertips, and the owl materialized, quiet for once. The eagle popped into view a few feet away.

Both flew after her as she crossed behind the castle's ruins.

Sean wanted to grab her, hold her tight, and never let go, but it wasn't how you sent soldiers into battle. Besides, once she started toward the old graveyard, she never looked back. He was at least twenty meters behind her when she ducked into one of the crumbling stone structures dotting perpetually wet grass. The eagle followed her inside.

The owl landed atop the crypt, fluffed its feathers around itself, and vanished from sight. Sean wasn't fooled. It would keep watch. If Liliana ran into problems, the bird was better positioned to reach her than he would be.

Kat and Arlen crawled into a nearby crypt. Smaller than the Cameron one, and in far worse repair, it smelled musty as he crouched to make his way through the partially fallen-in doorway.

"Over here," Arlen called softly.

Sean tripped over a pile of bones as he made his way to the side of the crypt nearest the Cameron final resting place. Druidic power lit the dank space, accompanied by a harsh, grinding noise.

"What are you doing?" Sean hissed, appalled. "No magic."

"All these old crypts had trap doors." Katerina turned and placed her mouth near his ear. "I found it, and Arlen opened it. Quicker route to Mom if we need one."

"I'm done." Arlen reeled in his power, and darkness claimed the crypt again.

Sean settled on his haunches and wove a subtle ward around them. If their situation hadn't been so serious, he'd have teased Arlen and Kat about their mutual love of rooting through dead things. Bones, artifacts, books, cultures. Both were anthropologists, and they lived for places like catacombs and mausoleums.

He waited, nerves riding a fine edge. He wanted to drape the goddamned Cameron crypt in magic. Something that would trip the moment Rhea showed up. If she sensed Druid magic, though, she either wouldn't show up...

Or she'd bring such an unholy host with her, they'd end up in a pitched confrontation they were likely to lose. Rhea wouldn't give a good goddamn about dragging monsters through a veil they had no business crossing. Or that major disturbances in the psychic balance might spell the end of human life on Earth.

Time dripped past. At least half an hour. Perhaps more.

"Do you think she won't come?" Kat whispered.

Sean had no idea, but the longer the interval grew, the more uncomfortable it made him. "Five more minutes," he said.

"Aye, and then what?" Arlen asked.

"We gather up Lil and return to Inverness."

"Mom wouldn't want us to do that," Kat argued, still whispering. "We have to let her call this. We can't give up for her."

Sean shut his jaws with a *clack* and curled his hands into fists. Why had he agreed with this plan? Surely, if they'd taken more time, another path would have shown itself.

One that didn't leave Liliana facing danger all alone.

So alert he was barely breathing, he felt a disturbance when it first washed over him. A light, exploratory touch that brushed their warding before retreating.

"She's here, or she soon will be." He kept his voice very low.

"Aye, I felt it too," Arlen growled.

Sean dropped to his belly and peered through the opening in the crypt's stone wall. Nothing had changed. The Cameron crypt looked the same, the owl still invisible. The same dark magic, stronger this time, rolled through the old graveyard, a murky cloud blotting out the night as it oozed through the far end of the Cameron crypt.

"It's her. Has to be." He wanted to use telepathy, but it took magic, and he couldn't risk it.

"Do ye suppose the rest of us felt it?" Arlen asked referring to the other Druids across the graveyard.

Sean had no idea, but he wasn't going to wait to make certain. He started out of the crypt, slithering on his belly, intent on reaching Liliana before Rhea discovered her deception and flattened the world with her fury. The owl, visible now, flew through the doorway.

Arlen and Kat crawled out behind him. They'd rehearsed the next part and remained shielded as they hurried into the Cameron crypt. Arlen had an iron blade, sheathed with magic. Once they dropped their warding, it would become visible.

The plan was to behead the witch and burn her bones.

At least this crypt allowed him to walk upright, except he was running rather than walking. Smoke rolled through the tight space, greasy and black and air-stealing. The owl had vanished, presumably to the lower level Kat described.

Not accessing magic beyond what little was required for their warding was an impediment. He stumbled over rocks and bones littering the floor, making enough noise to alert anyone who might be listening. The smoke thickened as he went deeper into the crypt.

No outraged howls rose from below.

Something was wrong. Rhea had to hear them. Why wasn't she reacting? And where the hell was all the smoke coming from? He tossed stealth to the four winds and kindled his power. It blazed with a blue-white light as he pounded down the last set of steps, coughing and choking.

The minute his warding fell, he knew they'd been outfoxed. Liliana's energy hung in the air, but she was gone. So was the owl. All that remained were air-stealing fumes. The smoke was magical, so he sent his own power to obliterate it.

A pitiful moan rose from Kat. "Goddammit. Where is she?"

The eagle, one wing hanging at an odd angle, the appendage clearly broken, lurched through a rent in the ether cawing imprecations. *"Gone. Gone. Smoke. Fire. Gone."*

"Gone where?" Sean shouted, too desolate to

worry about modulating his tone. The bird didn't answer.

Katerina scooped her familiar out of the air and held it close.

Footsteps pounded as Gloria, followed by the other Druids, ran toward them through the thinning web of smoke.

Sean ignored them all, chanting furiously as he summoned a portal. Liliana's magical signature was fresh, possible to follow, but he had to hurry.

"I'm coming with you," Arlen announced.

"As am I." Gloria threaded her power with his.

"This is my fault," Katerina said. "I should go."

"Nay, lass." Arlen leveled his gaze on her. "I love you, but ye'd be naught but an impediment."

"Agreed," Gloria said brusquely. "See to your bird. It needs your energy to mend itself."

Morgan strode to Arlen's side. "If I come, we'll be four. Once we locate Liliana, 'twill make five. Odd numbers have transformative power, and we'll need every edge we can lay our hands on."

Magic boiled and bubbled around Sean. His spell was nearly ready. "Come close," he instructed through clenched teeth, "and we'll be gone from here."

He held himself together by the thinnest of margins. He had no idea where the casting would take him. He'd instructed it to follow Liliana's magic like a homing pigeon. No matter where he ended up, though, even in the bowels of Hell, he'd fight for the woman he loved.

Fight and win, he told himself. Liliana would not die at the hands of her Roskelly ancestors. Or be turned to dark power, either.

CHAPTER 13

*L*iliana was too nervous to sit, so she paced up and down the lower level of the Cameron crypt. Every once in a while, she flipped a braid forward, checking to make certain her hair was still red. As a witch, her night vision was decent, and Sean had been clear about not employing any magic at all beyond her glamour.

She talked out loud as she trod up and down the crypt. This level held older remains, mostly bones laid out on slabs. Any accessories they'd taken into Death's realm with them had long since been pilfered. While her daughter lived for places like this, Liliana had always preferred working with the living.

She tried for a believable monologue.

"This is the same spot you found me last time," she began. "I've seen the light. Mom and Gran, they lied to me. No one ever told me I was a witch. Not until you forced their hand. Hell, they led me to believe you were crazy."

With the eagle perched on her shoulder, she continued her transit of the underground space. "In any event, I like magic. A lot. I'm ready to claim my heritage. If it's not too late."

She fell silent before repeating the essence of her words. After the third round, she started to wonder if Rhea was going to respond. She'd had plenty of opportunity. She might not be paying attention, but Liliana didn't think that was it.

More likely, her grandmother was done with all of them—unless you counted her summoning demons and dragons and going on an all-out attack. She clasped her hands behind her back to resist the temptation to use her power. What she really wanted to do was talk with Sean telepathically—plot out their next moves—but telepathy was off the table for now.

How long should she wait?

It had been more than half an hour. Maybe as much as forty-five minutes. Part of her—a pretty goddamned big part—was within a hairsbreadth of packing up and leaving. They'd have to try something else.

The eagle's talons tightened on her shoulder. Was

it reacting to her thoughts—and telling her leaving was a bad idea? Or had it felt something?

She unclasped her hands and stood at the end of the crypt waiting. Not using magic was tough. She was used to augmenting her senses with her paranormal ability.

With almost zero warning, a tsunami of dark power steamrolled down the stairs, filling the crypt's lowest level with fiery smoke. It seared her lungs and made her eyes water. She stared through the murk, searching for Rhea's long silver-black hair and aquamarine eyes.

If the old witch was present, she was concealing herself.

The eagle squawked, hanging on for dear life, about the time her owl shot through flames and landed on her other shoulder chittering at the eagle in little, high-pitched hoots. Liliana didn't require her familiar to spell things out. She shucked the glamor and threw her magic wide-open, intent on teleporting out of the crypt. Whatever was happening down here was bad. Somehow, Rhea had figured out she'd been duped, and was on the warpath.

The smoke thickened, eating up what little oxygen remained. She needed to breathe to work magic. Before the thick murk totally obscured everything, she groped her way toward where she remembered the stairs were.

"I don't think so, *Liliana*," was followed by a pitiful shriek from the eagle. It let go of her shoulder and vanished.

"If you hurt Kat's familiar," she rasped, throat raw from inhaling smoke.

"Ye're scarcely in a bargaining position. Lying, conniving bitch."

"Like you're any better," Liliana shot back. "You killed my husband."

"Ye're who married a mortal. What did ye expect? They're weak. Although"—another cackle—"he was delightful while he lasted. Sweet. Succulent."

Fury battered Liliana, but she couldn't do anything about it. Lungs seizing, she dropped to the ground. If any air remained, it would be here. Her head spun as she dragged herself forward using her flagging power to concentrate the air into something breathable. She'd just reached the steps, clawing at them for purchase, when everything went totally dark.

She fell backward, spinning and flopping, as her body plunged through blackness. The owl was still with her, its magic encased deep within. Her last thoughts before consciousness fled were she hoped to hell Sean would give her at least some time to find her own way back.

If he galloped after her in a misplaced Sir Galahad move, Rhea would kill him, laughing all the while.

Thank all the blessed gods and goddesses it was her and not Kat shooting through time to goddess only knew where.

The last thought jolted through her, and she forced herself to remain awake. She had one chance to push her own magic into the spell carrying her away. That chance was now. If she didn't jump on it, it would be too late.

For all she knew, Rhea was pissed enough to send her back to the Pleistocene. With the owl helping, she dissected the spell that had trapped her, traced the location vector, and pushed late 1800s Inverness into its place. She considered California but wasn't certain her magical reserves could pervert the spell to that extent.

Panting and gasping, she wrapped her arms around herself and introduced more power into Rhea's casting a little bit at a time. Finally certain she'd done all she could, she waited, breath wheezing from her damaged lungs. Smoke still coated her nose and mouth and made her cough.

Doesn't matter. I'm alive. And I'll find my way back to Sean.

Whatever she did, she'd have to be quick about it. Rhea could find her, track her by her blood, but at least she'd bought herself a respite. Assuming she didn't fall into some churchman's arms the second she dropped out of the time spell. Not one to repeat her errors, she took care and shrouded herself in invisibility. It would give her an edge, conceal her from anyone who'd turn her in to another iteration of Father Abernathy.

She kept expecting gray to streak the black surrounding her, but it didn't happen. Too much time had passed. Far too much. Where the hell was Rhea's spell taking her? Why hadn't her attempt to alter it worked the way it should have?

"Can you break us out of this?" the owl asked.

She didn't waste breath inquiring what it knew. She'd already determined the enchantment wasn't what she'd thought. Encased in a lightless void, spinning, tumbling, she feared Rhea had consigned her to a perpetually moving prison.

One with no easy way out.

Worse, a place no one could find her, either.

If she stepped back a few paces, moved away from the horror and dread filling her, she had to offer her grandmother credit for what could easily be the final solution to rid herself of a witch she considered a traitor.

She couldn't do anything flopping from side to side. She'd curled into a ball with her arms around her bent legs, but it didn't keep her in a stable position. Absent stability, the spell ingredients she had with her would fall out of reach as soon as she extracted them.

Never mind being able to mix anything or hit the side of a barn door with the amount of power needed to ignite everything into a mixture powerful enough to blast her and the owl out of their predicament.

Liliana released her clasped hands and reached her arms outward, legs too, but they didn't contact anything solid. Determined, she mimicked a swimmer's motions, trying for a straight line. It was almost impossible. The rolling, pitching movement of whatever held her captive tossed her from front to back and side to side.

Teeth gritted, breath tight in her chest, she made another attempt. And another.

"*No!*" The owl's voice was sharp. "*To your right. You keep missing it.*"

"Of course, I keep missing anything useful. I can't see."

"*I can't either,*" her familiar retorted, "*but something feels different on that side.*"

Right turned to left and then to above her before her fingertips grazed something solid. With a determined heave, she threw her body after her extended arm until she connected with a rough, curved surface. Panting from effort, throat dry and raw from smoke, she ran her hands over the barrier. Solid in places, squishy in others, it reminded her of the way bodies rotted.

The image was so disquieting, she quashed it. If her cage was made of the decomposing bodies of Rhea's enemies, she didn't need to think about it. The soft spots gave her purchase. She jammed a boot toe into one, kicking with the other foot until she found a second notch just at the limit of her spread legs.

Her hand crunched through something that gave off a noxious smell, but she had three points of attachment. Clinging like a limpet, she lay against the curvature of the wall. She hadn't realized until then how disorienting it was to not know which way she'd be tossed next.

Once she'd caught her breath, she understood that while she may have solved one problem—the perpetual motion one—she wasn't much closer to the static position she needed to cast a counterspell. For that, she needed her hands. And she needed to be facing outward, back against the wall.

Rope was the answer, except she hadn't brought any.

Careful not to drop anything, she transferred the linen square with her spell ingredients from her cloak to a skirt pocket. Next came the bit of timber from Sean's castle—and the vial of his blood.

Was that what had given her away?

It didn't matter. What did was getting out of here before she grew weak from no water or food. With her free hand, she removed her cloak from her shoulders and wedged it between her body and the wall, wrapping one end around a thigh for good measure. If the garment dropped into the whirling abyss beneath her, she'd never find it.

She tugged a dirk from its sheath around one thigh. She didn't usually carry weapons, but Sean had insisted. A slow, sad tide moved through her as she thought of him. He would have gone after her by now, and his magic probably wasn't working any better than her attempt to pervert Rhea's spell had gone.

Panic gripped her that they'd played right into Rhea's hands.

Christ! I have to get out of here. Have to warn everyone.

Her vision hazed with reddish-gray, but the relentless black surrounding her didn't budge. She turned her attention to the cloak and her knife and cut two wide strips on a bias to keep the finely woven wool from unraveling and becoming useless.

Once she had them, she secured the strips around her waist and what remained of the cloak around her neck. That done, she sheathed the knife and searched for something to tie herself to.

Everything took forever. She was clumsy, mostly because hanging onto the wall was her top priority—for now. She had to move her stance twice before she located what she'd been looking for: a place where the solid portion of wall was only a few inches across with squishy places on both sides.

Ungainly, like a beached whale, she threaded one end of the torn cloak from her waist through the soft spots. Her fingers slimed with goo that stank of death and rot. So did the wool once she dragged it around. She repeated the process with the second length of her cloak until both dangled, ends hanging loose.

Still facing the wall, she reached behind herself and tied a loose knot in first one strip, and then the next.

Careful not to dislodge anything, she turned until her back was flat against the wall. Then she tightened one length of wool, knotting it over her belly. She wanted to screech her success, but she knew better. She may have accomplished step one, but she was a very long way from victory.

She wanted to take a break, but it was a bad idea. Something about the spinning prison held a hypnotic aspect. If she gave in to it, she might never regain the determination burning through her. She snugged the second piece of cloak around her hips. Between the two, they held her firmly to the wall.

As secure as she was likely to get, she turned her attention inward. "I'll need your help."

"I will make my magic available, but you must hurry."

A sense of something imminent and deadly hurtling toward them pricked at the edges of her mind. Still far away, it was moving closer. She'd been so intent on stabilizing herself, she hadn't noticed it until now.

She reached into a pocket and closed her hand around the square of linen. What spell should she employ? She wouldn't get a second chance if she chose wrong. Liliana cursed herself for her almost total inattention to her magical side. She may have owned her power, but it didn't mean she was competent wielding it.

"Should I try a time-travel spell?" she asked her familiar.

"No. Those only work if you know where you are."

"If not that, then what?" She held her breath. Would her familiar be able to bail them out? Make up for her shortcomings in the magical realm?

"Two choices. Use Sean's blood to shape a seeking spell. It will take you to him—even if he's dead."

"What's the other?" she asked through chattering teeth.

"Use the wood from his home to shape the same seeking spell. It's far safer."

The bird stopped there. Regardless of what

happened to her, the owl could return to its realm. "Thank you." Her tone was formal. "I will create my spell with Sean's blood. If Rhea captured him, I owe it to him to do everything I can to free him."

"*I respect your choice.*" The owl's response was equally formal.

"I release you if you choose to leave."

"*Do you want me to go?*" The owl punctuated its question with a soft hoot.

"No, but it's not fair for me to select a risky path and drag you along."

More hoots. "*I accept the challenge.*" The owl emerged, talons digging into her shoulder.

Liliana stroked its feathers. Emotion rocked her, narrowing her throat, but she refocused fast. Malevolence was closing in on them. It wasn't in a rush. Why should it be? It figured they were sitting ducks. And they would have been if she hadn't had the presence of mind to bring a few witchy trappings along.

Thank the goddess for small favors.

The seeking spell was one of the simplest castings. She began to chant softly as she instructed one end of the torn cloak to form a bowl. Tipping ingredients into it, she let the spell build around her. Her magic wasn't as strong as she would have liked, but she didn't want to tip off whatever was hovering in the wings that she was trying to bolt.

The last ingredient was Sean's blood. Liliana took a deep, steadying breath. She'd empty the vial and throw her magic wide open all in one fell swoop, igniting her escape hatch. Would it be enough?

It has to be.

Believe, she instructed herself in the same strict tones she used when she lectured medical students to never lose their compassion.

Liliana stabilized her makeshift container with one hand. She pulled the stopper from the vial with her teeth, poured Sean's blood over the bubbling mass, and shouted the final Gaelic words to kindle her casting.

The owl's power spilled through her like warm honey. She wove it in with her own, working fast. A distant roar filled her ears. Was it her casting taking hold? Or was it the bad thing ready to rain disaster on her head?

"Focus!" The owl screeched and vanished inside her.

She did. Visualized her spell taking her to Sean. Pictured her prison walls breaking apart and her arrowing directly to Sean's side, wherever he'd ended up. After a heart-stopping moment when the oily taint of evil came so close she could feel fire licking at her heels, she dug deep.

Gave it everything she had and then some.

With an ear-splitting crack, the black fell away, and she hurtled through gray mist. The haze thinned, and she shaped magic into a barrier to both cushion her fall and confer invisibility. Just in time because moments later she bounced into an open courtyard surrounded by high walls. Gallows and stocks lined one side. Latin filled her ears.

Fuck. Another goddess-be-damned church.

She stumbled to her feet, trying not to raise dust or make any noise that would alert the clergy milling about to her presence. She couldn't see through the black-robed men, so she worked her way to a better vantage point. Sean had to be here. Her spell had run true, so why couldn't she see him?

The tall, tonsured monk blocking her vision moved aside, dragged his cock out, and pissed into the dirt.

Liliana stifled a gasp. Arlen, Morgan, and Gloria stood immobile, wrapped in lengths of heavy chain. Sean lay on the ground, equally hobbled. Despair threatened to swamp her. Was he dead? She had to find out, so she sent a jolt of magic forward. Not a lot, but enough to determine if he was still breathing.

"What was that?" a priest asked in fractured English. English with a definite Scottish burr. A heavy gold cross set with glowing gems hung from his neck.

Liliana ducked behind a row of clerics, peering

between two of them. She'd been stupid to deploy power. A fucking fool. That priest was a Hunter, and the jewels in his cross were keyed to witch power.

"Och, damn if the wee holy man dinna catch me out," Gloria crooned in a bitch of a Scottish accent.

"No more!" The priest shook his cross at her, but she laughed in his face.

Did she know Liliana was here? She'd almost have to. Gloria had always had power to burn, plenty to run rings around everyone else.

"Get on with the hangings," another priest cried.

A susurrus of anticipation swelled through the crowd, reminding her how bloody and unprincipled the church had been. The unprincipled part hadn't changed much, but at least they'd stopped murdering those they considered anathema to Christian principles.

Only because they can't get away with it anymore.

On that cheerful note, she stepped away from the clerics sheltering her from the Hunter and his glowing stones. He'd assume Gloria was the element kicking off his early-warning witch radar.

It might give Liliana the edge she needed, but whether she could defeat four sets of chains before the clerics milling about the courtyard reacted remained to be seen. The biggest element in her favor was fear. Churchmen—along with everyone else from what she presumed was the middle of the eighteenth century or thereabouts—were deathly afraid of magic.

She got as close as she dared, so near she could have touched Gloria, and began the subtle threads of an unmaking spell. Latin droned around her as she worked. She wanted to check on Sean again, but the rise and fall of his chest was reassuring.

Damn Rhea. She'd consigned Liliana to what she assumed would be certain death, while sending Sean and the others on a wild goose chase that landed them squarely in mortal danger.

If she got out of the current mess, she wouldn't rest until Rhea was deader than dead. The owl hooted agreement from the spot inside her where it had taken refuge after her seeking spell took off.

Another hoot came from the top of the courtyard's spiked gates. Her familiar settled in plain view, fluffing its feathers around it.

Arlen glanced its way. His eyes widened. Morgan smiled.

Gloria cackled, sounding like the witch she was.

It provided a diversion, and Liliana fed magic into her fledgling spell.

The Hunter cut the flow of Latin spewing from his mouth long enough to shout, "I told ye. No more, witch."

"Ye're about to hang me. I'll do what I want."

Pride rolled through Liliana. Her bitchy, always-had-to-be-right mother had steel balls. The least she could do was free her. Amid clanging and clattering, Gloria's shackles fell to the ground.

The Hunter's eyes widened until white showed all around the dark irises. "How did ye do that?"

"Wouldn't ye like to know?"

On the heels of Gloria's challenge, a wave of Druidic magic rolled through the stockade walls. A section crashed inward, and a dozen mounted Druids galloped through, swords swinging.

Liliana whooped triumphantly and raced toward Sean. Magic crackling ahead of her, she cut through his chains and fell to her knees next to him. He was breathing. He had to be all right.

When she laid her hands on him, intent on assessing damage, he was burning up with fever. What the hell? He must have an infection, but where?

"I'm here, child." Gloria squatted on Liliana's other side.

Liliana dropped the invisibility cloaking her. "What happened to him?"

"Black power. Rhea wedged something into his magical center. She did battle with him just before she dumped the lot of us here."

"We have to get him home. Or at least somewhere I can work on him." Liliana ran her hands down his body, hunting for other injuries and not finding any.

"If we try to drag him through time, we'll kill him." Gloria's blue-green gaze was grim.

The sounds of battle rose around them. Screams. Groans. Death rattles. The stench of spilled entrails and blood thickened.

Good. Liliana hoped every one of the bloodthirsty priests met a grisly end.

Arlen ran lightly to them and knelt next to Sean. Power flashed from him, and he winced. "He's dying."

"Tell me something I don't know," Gloria snapped.

"Hurry, Mom." Desperation swept through Liliana. "Get us somewhere I can work on him."

"Go. Morgan and I will find our way back. Everything's under control here, thanks to the Druids heeding my call," Arlen said.

Gloria's spell settled around Liliana where she cradled Sean against her body, willing his fever to at least slow down. She locked gazes with Arlen. "We are mated. It may help. I'll do everything I can to save him."

"I know ye will, lass." Arlen straightened. "Goddess's grace be with you."

The churchyard with its stench of righteous entitlement faded. A grotto complete with a pool formed around them. "Quick," Liliana instructed.

"Help me get him into the water. It will give us a chance of controlling the fever until we can locate whatever Rhea marked him with."

"I hope it's that simple," Gloria muttered as they submerged Sean to his neck, holding his head out of the water.

"What do you mean?"

"Let's hope he's still whole once we've removed the Black Witch taint."

"I'm his mate, Mother. Surely I can replace whatever he needs."

Gloria settled a hand on her shoulder briefly, but her eyes reflected worry.

And sorrow.

"Goddammit, Mother. Believe in me. In us."

"I do, Liliana. And I'll help every way I can."

Sean wandered through a macabre landscape. Battles raged around him. Harsh. Bloody. Ephemeral. Every time he tried to join one, the scene shifted. He drew a hand across his forehead. He was hot. So hot. And tired.

Weary to his bones, but he knew instinctively that if he gave in, laid down, he'd die. His head was fuzzy, but he forced himself to remember what had happened. He'd crafted a seeking spell, intent on following Liliana. Instead, he'd run up against Rhea in a pulsating darkness, narrow enough to impede maneuvering.

Arlen had been there. Morgan too. But Arlen's sword had been useless. He'd swung it and swung it. Each time, Rhea dodged the blow. Hemmed in by her magic, their Druid power was laughable. Gloria wasn't anywhere in sight. He heard her, though, screaming curses as she tried to batter her way through to them.

In a single, coordinated motion, Rhea had surged forward and slammed the flat of her hand against his chest. Pain rocketed through him. If she'd sent a multi-edged burning blade through his ribs, it couldn't have hurt any worse.

The black funnel vanished, replaced by a churchyard. He'd lost consciousness about the time a flock of clerics mobbed them, but not before he realized Rhea had thrown them to the wolves and vanished.

Big surprise. Witches didn't fare any better with churchmen than Druids.

All that was gone now. The church and angry monks had faded to nothingness. Arlen was gone. So was Morgan. And the fire burning through his body, searing his flesh, only grew hotter. What had Rhea done to him? Sent him on a one-way journey to Hell?

He thought he'd sensed Liliana, but he must have been wrong. She was lost too. Unless maybe she'd made her way back to his castle. He hoped so. He wanted her to live...

Goddess's tits. Nothing made sense. His mind had devolved into a wandering jumble of randomly firing neurons.

I need to hang on.

But it was too much trouble. Too hard.

His body bumped over an uneven surface. He tried to scream, but he couldn't even open his mouth. The pain factor escalated until agony and suffering were the only things in his universe. His body was on fire. Heated nails drove into his brain. He couldn't think. Couldn't see.

He hunted for his magical center, but the quest took far too much effort.

The journey over whatever was tearing the hell out of his back stopped abruptly. Something dense surrounded him. Dense and mercifully cold. After a pathetically long while, he understood he'd been dragged into a pool of water. He had to have been dragged because he'd stopped moving anywhere under his own steam a while ago.

Or maybe he'd imagined the whole thing. Nothing was real. Not anymore.

"*Sean!*" rattled through his brain.

He searched for words to tell whoever it was to leave him be, but both Gaelic and English had deserted him, along with all the other languages he spoke.

"Sean! Goddammit, Sean. You cannot check out. I won't let you." Someone gave his shoulders a good, hard shake.

He flinched. This wasn't telepathy. No magic here. They were words. Real words. Who'd spoken them? He opened his mouth, tried to ask, but nothing came out. It was as if someone had inserted a big fat disconnect between his brain and the rest of his body.

I'm dying. This is how it happens. From the arms and legs inward.

He sagged into the water. If it covered his face, he could hurry things along. He could at least do that much, but hands held his head above the waterline, and he was too weak to pull it out of their grip.

"We can't, it's too risky," someone female said.

"We have to, Mom. No choice," another woman cut in.

"Sean!" The second voice, the one also talking with her mum, sounded rattled but determined. "It's Liliana. Rhea planted a splinter of evil in your magical center. Mother is with me, and we have to take it out. It's going to hurt like a bitch, but if we don't remove it, you'll die."

Liliana?

He had to be hallucinating. Along with dying. His brain was playing tricks on him, before it failed entirely. He struggled against the hands holding his head, tried his damnedest to pry his eyes open.

No dice.

"On my count of three," the first voice said. "One, two...and now."

The scream he hadn't been able to find earlier shot from his mouth, followed by so many more he lost count. His back bowed in agony. His heels kicked the bottom of the pool. Waves of anguish rolled through him, starting in the center of his chest and not missing a single cell on their way through.

"Aw, Jesus. I'm sorry, so sorry." The second voice cracked with emotion. "Just a little more. We're almost there."

"I can take this next part." Voice number one sounded gravelly but gentle.

"No. It'll go faster with us both."

His body was still vibrating from the last onslaught. He tried to gird himself, but it was as hopeless as opening his eyes. At least this time, he was expecting the blast of witch power that scoured him from head to foot.

Wait a minute.

Witch power.

He'd recognized its distinct feel. Maybe Liliana really was here. And the mother she was talking with was Gloria. He hurt too much to sort things out. By the balls of every Druid who'd ever lived, he hurt, but it was lessening. While still white-hot, agony wasn't washing him away, obliterating everything he was.

Pain ripped through him a few more times before it simmered down to serious discomfort.

"Damn, I do believe we've done it," voice one—Gloria?—said.

"I hope so. I can't put him through another round of that."

Hands ran the length of his body, lingering mid-chest, the same spot Rhea had targeted. It felt raw, as if he'd lost flesh down to his ribs, but he had to be imagining it.

He groaned. Maybe his screams had paved the way for his voice to return.

Arms gathered him close, held him. Liliana's familiar scent filled his nostrils. It took gargantuan effort, but he lifted an arm from the water and placed it on top of hers.

"We can get him out of the pool," voice one said briskly.

"It served its purpose. His fever is nearly gone," Liliana agreed.

"The water was ancillary. His fever is gone because we defeated Rhea's enchantment."

"We won, Mother. Don't pick it to shreds."

If he could have smiled, he would have. No one bickered quite like Lil and her mum. Feathers brushed his face, so the familiars must be flitting about. He wanted to thank everyone, but his tongue felt thick and stupid. At least he had a sense of it again as four hands half-carried and half-dragged him onto rocky dirt.

Maybe telepathy would work. It didn't require much magic. *"Liliana? Gloria?"* he croaked.

"Yes, love. Both of us are here."

"*Where is here?*"

"The closest safe spot where we could work on you," Liliana replied. "You nearly died on me."

He chuckled. "*Och and tell me aught I doona know.*"

More dragging. This time they propped him against a large, flat rock. He inhaled to the bottom of his lungs. It hurt like a bitch, but he did it again for good measure. After a few more deep breaths, he willed his eyes to open, and they obeyed him.

It took a few moments for the world to swim into focus. Liliana sat on one side of him, Gloria on the other. Their familiars rode on their shoulders, and mage lights floated above them. Since his body was returning to his control, he struggled to form words. "Where are we?" He'd asked before, but they hadn't answered.

Liliana glanced at her mum and raised a dark brow.

"We're in Inverness, around 1780 or 90, or thereabouts. We got lucky with this cave. Its waters are said to have healing properties. I was prepared to chase people out and wipe memories, but I didn't have to."

"Thank you. Both of you. All of you." He included the birds and tried to sit up straighter.

"Uh-uh." Liliana rested both hands on his

shoulders. "Not yet. You have a hell of a hole in your chest. It needs to knit back together a little more."

He tilted his chin down, trying to look, but all he saw was his blood-soaked shirt and tartan.

"You'll have to take my word for it." Liliana pulled her brows together. "I'm afraid I made a bit of a mess, but I had to hurry. That thing was eating up your magic and killing you."

"Christ, lassie. Doona apologize for saving my life." He resisted the urge to touch the wound, explore its boundaries with his fingers.

Leaning forward, Gloria peered at his soaked tartan and the linen shirt beneath. "It's looking better, coming together faster than I expected. What do you think?" she asked Liliana. "You're the doctor."

Liliana narrowed her eyes and lifted a hand over the center of his chest. A cut place ran through the meaty part of her thumb, and blood dripped into his wound. His skin burned, but then warmed as her blood joined with his.

"Good enough for us to leave. I've got him." Liliana wrapped her arms around his shoulders. This time, he was able to hug her back.

"I'll handle the spell." Witch magic built around them as Gloria summoned a time portal to return them home.

Home.

He held onto Liliana and thanked every god and goddess in the Celtic pantheon. He'd truly been only a few breaths from death. He hadn't imagined it. Blind, deaf, wandering through memories, he'd written off ever seeing his home again.

Or everyone he loved.

The curved walls of the cave fell away, replaced by the whitewashed plaster of his great room. A fire crackled in the hearth, and everyone circled around him, kneeling to be at floor level.

He tried for jaunty, but emotion ran far too near the surface. "I'm grateful," he managed. "For every one of you."

"Probably not as grateful as I am to see you alive." Arlen gripped Sean's upper arm. "When the women left with you, I'd not have given two coppers for your chances."

Sean inhaled raggedly. "Oh ye of little faith."

"'Twasn't that at all, and ye know it. I felt the life seeping from you and couldn't do aught to stem the tide."

Katerina wrapped her arms around Liliana from behind. "Mom. Oh, Mom. I was so afraid I'd lost you." Tears spilled down her face.

Liliana let go of Sean and twisted around, so she could hug her daughter. "I'm tougher than you give me credit for, but I have to admit it was rough out there. Nip and tuck, and then some."

"It should have been me—" Kat began.

"No." Liliana cut her off. "You'd have been lost in the vortex that imprisoned me. As it was, it took every shred of my magic to free myself."

"Someday," Kat said.

Liliana nodded. "Yes. Someday, you'll be strong enough, but it wasn't today."

Gloria dragged Katerina upright. "You can visit with us later. We need to get Sean out of those wet clothes and into bed."

Sean struggled to his feet, determined to make it to his rooms under his own power. He was feeling stronger, the danger of dying a thing of the past.

"We're good, Mom." Liliana got to her feet.

"Are you sure?" Gloria asked.

"Yeah. Maybe heat some soup."

"I can do that, and spell it with magic so it stays hot." Gloria turned and walked slowly toward the kitchens.

Liliana stood by Sean's side. He leaned on her, and together they walked slowly from the room, the hum of conversation following them. A whoosh and a blur of feathers, and the owl flew past, hooting softly.

Long before they made the end of the hall, he knew he'd overestimated his strength, but he refused to give up. The door to his rooms grew incrementally closer. By the time they got there, his legs were shaking.

"Stubborn, stubborn man," Liliana murmured, "but I love that part of you. If you weren't so pigheaded, you'd be dead." She led him through the door and kicked it shut behind them. "Stand still while I undress you."

She started by unlacing his soft, knee-high boots. Absent the lacings, they fell away.

Next, she unwound the tartan and drew the shirt over his head. "Hold up one more minute," she said and ran to turn the duvet down. A quick trip to the bathroom yielded a soft terrycloth towel that she laid across the sheets to soak up any residual moisture.

He crossed the room, aware of each step, and let himself gingerly down onto the bed. She moved his legs onto the mattress and covered him with the duvet. "Sleep, love. It's the best thing. I'll be here in case you need anything."

The owl perched on the footboard, regarding him sagely with its amber eyes.

He tried again for words to tell her how much he loved her and appreciated her and what an incredible woman she was and how fortunate he was that she was his. Despite his good intentions, all he got out was, "I love you, *mo croix*," before sleep felled him like a tree toppling onto its side in a thick forest.

Every time he woke, she was next to him on the bed or sitting on a small divan near it. She offered soup, wine, water, and a few more drops of her healing blood.

Light streamed through his windows when he finally opened his eyes and knew that this time they'd remain open. His head felt clear, his body strong.

Liliana got up from the sofa and perched on the side of his bed. "Back with the living, are you?"

"Firmly." He grinned. "How long did I sleep?"

She shrugged. "The better part of three days."

His eyebrows shot upward. "That long?"

"Yup. Oh, you got up a time or two, and I've been feeding you and keeping you hydrated. Once you even took a quick shower, but I knew the healing wasn't complete, and I spelled you back to sleep."

"So 'tis your doing I slept so long."

"A bit self-serving on my part since I wanted to make certain you were well and truly healed with no residual damage." She laced her fingers in with his. "It's a nice day, chilly but the sun's been peeking through. Feel like a walk outside?"

"A most excellent idea." He opened his arms, and she snuggled into them. He angled his head and kissed her, loving how her mouth softened beneath his, how her body molded to his.

His cock stirred, and he broke the kiss. "If you want that stroll, we should leave now."

A soft smile illuminated her features. "Right you are. See? Told you shepherding you back to health was self-serving on my part."

He grinned. "Lusty wench."

"We're the best kind." She scrambled off the bed. "Let me find you some clothes."

He tossed the covers aside, aware of her eyes on him as he pulled on black sweatpants and a stretchy shirt, topped by a thick, flannel jacket. Socks and running shoes followed. "Is anyone else still here, or is it just us?"

"They all went home. Even Mom. She's back in Nevada, but she'll return tonight or tomorrow morning." Liliana slipped into one of his cable-knit cardigans and wrapped a hand around his arm.

Together, they walked through a glass door at the far end of his suite of rooms that opened onto a terrace and thence into lush gardens. Maintained with magic, they bloomed year around. He breathed deep. Nothing like chill, damp marine air to clear his head and his heart.

"I have a few questions," he said after they'd made a full transit of the castle grounds.

"I figured you would." She smiled at him. "It's why we're out here walking and not rolling around in your bed."

"That part will happen soon."

Her grin expanded. "I'll hold you to it." After a brief pause, she added, "About those questions…"

"How'd you end up where I was? Did you use my blood?"

Liliana nodded. "I did. The short version is Rhea captured me, but rather than sending me backward in time, I was suspended in a whirling, tumbling capsule. I still have no idea where I was. It could have been a borderworld or somewhere a few hundred feet above Earth.

"It took time to establish a stable platform. More time to get a spell together. My bird was with me, and it told me to use a seeking spell, not a time-travel one."

"Wise of it," he agreed. "You need to know both starting and ending points to build a time vortex."

"I know that now. All the while I've been playing doctor, watching over you, I've also been studying. You'll find a pile of sourcebooks and scrolls next to my sofa." Her smile was replaced by thin-lipped determination. "I have years of neglect to make up for, but I'll never go into another conflict as magically inept as I've become."

He stopped walking and gathered her into his arms. "One of my last thoughts was that I hoped you were safe."

A corner of her mouth twisted into a lopsided expression. "Funny, you were in my thoughts as well.

Once I knew I'd be casting a seeking spell, I had two choices—"

"Me or this castle." He finished her sentence.

Liliana nodded. "Exactly. I picked you. Damned good thing too. If I'd teleported to the castle, you'd be dead."

His heart swelled with emotion until it cracked wide open. She'd chosen him over safety. "You should have—"

She shook her head and put a hand over his mouth. "I know what you're about to say, and it's bullshit. In the same situation, you'd have found your way to me, not a safe haven."

"You're absolutely correct, *léannan.*"

"I know. Anyway, Rhea did a number on us. She thought she'd moved me out of the way—permanently. And then, she tossed the rest of you into a situation where she was fairly certain you'd end up swinging from gibbets. If Arlen hadn't called in Druid reinforcements, I'm not at all certain I'd have had enough magic to break everyone's chains."

He cupped her chin in a hand. "You're a brave woman. Resourceful as hell."

She made a face and switched to Gaelic. "Aye, but Rhea is still on the rampage. She must know I escaped, and all the rest of us too."

He'd already thought of that. "We'll figure something out."

"We have to. Arlen's called a general gathering two nights hence on South Ronaldsay Island. All the Druids in this region—and three witches."

"I'll talk with him later today. See what he has in mind." Sean pushed dark strands of hair away from Liliana's lovely face. Her skin felt like silk beneath his fingertips.

"One of the agenda items is formalizing our marriage." Her smile returned. "Speaking of which, it was a damned good idea on your part. The linkage helped me pull you back from the edge of the abyss." She shook her head, a faraway look in her green eyes. "Funny how nothing in our lives is coincidental. If it weren't for my work with the dying, I wouldn't have had such a clear recognition of the liminal place that separates our world from what comes next."

"When I spoke the Druid vows," he said slowly and deliberately, "I did so because I knew you were the one woman for me. Whom I'd been waiting for. Certainty ran through me like quicksilver, and I couldn't not have uttered the words to bind you to me."

"Like I said, nothing is coincidental. Ready to go back inside?"

He pressed his lips to her forehead and then both

cheeks before brushing them across her mouth. "Never readier."

As they walked through the gardens, flowers bloomed around them, responding to their joy. Retracing their steps, they ducked through the terrace door that led directly to his rooms. Liliana pushed the door shut and followed him through the small study and into his bedroom, dropping clothes in her wake.

When he turned around, intent on undressing her, she was already naked. A satisfied, very male sound bubbled from him. "I seem to be a wee bit behind the curve," he said and toed off his shoes.

"I got pretty good at taking your clothes off." She ran her tongue over her lower lip. "But it would be fun to watch you undress."

"Och, so now I'm a Chippendale model?" he teased as he draped his jacket across a chair back, following it with his shirt.

"They could never in a million years be as stunning as you. Do you realize you're shining? Magic is spilling from you and lighting up my heart. And my life."

He crossed to where she stood, arms open. She ran lightly into them and hugged him, hands splayed across his back. Sean closed his mouth over hers. Power was indeed sheeting from him, and he wrapped them both in his joy. He'd come home, found everything he'd ever wanted and more.

He tore his mouth from hers long enough to say, "Ye're never leaving my side again, lassie. Not now. Not ever."

"You won't get any arguments from me. We're stronger together. Now, can we get those pants off you?"

Laughter rolled from a happy place. "You're always wanting me naked."

"Do I hear a complaint?"

Instead of answering, he directed a thread of magic to push his sweatpants out of the way. Skin-to-skin, he pressed the length of his body against her velvety flesh and walked them near enough the bed to tumble into it.

Surrounded by heat, sensation, and desire, love rushed through him as he claimed the woman in his arms with his body, his heart, and his soul. Trials lay ahead. Major ones, but they were stronger together than apart.

That strength wouldn't fail, and he'd make certain they staked out the future they deserved. One where they weren't always one step ahead of the latest Roskelly plot to resurrect their Black Witch bloodlines...

Liliana sank her teeth into his shoulder.

Sean laughed again. "Did I miss a wee bit of vampire skulking in your blood, *léannan?*"

She tilted her head. "Your attention was, um, wavering. I merely intended to bring it fully back into this bed. And me."

He wrapped an arm around her and smoothed strands of dark hair away from her face. "'Tis my nature to worry, lass. And to plan. Blame it on my Scottish roots, but point taken." He brushed his thumb over her full lower lip. "I love you."

Warmth spilled from her green eyes. "I love you too. We'll get through this. Just because we haven't trounced Rhea and my other dead witchy kinswomen yet doesn't mean it's not possible."

"Now whose attention is wandering?" He snugged her close, cock jammed against her belly.

"Not mine." Reaching between them, she curved her fingers around his erection.

Her touch was electric, enticing. His heart hit triple-time rhythm, and his throat clotted with desire. Words failed him, so he crushed his lips over hers. The woman in his arms meant everything to him. He'd protect her, care for her, shelter their bairns when they came along.

She shifted beneath him and wrapped her legs around his waist, the invitation unmistakable. She still had hold of him, and he let her guide him to her hot, slick entrance. After ripping his mouth from hers, he supported his upper body on his arms and slid into her in a single, sure, hard thrust.

Savage possessiveness swept through him, and he rasped, "Ye're mine, lass. Mine. Now and forever more."

"I could say the same. We belong to each other." She bumped her hips upward.

The vista of her coal-black hair, heated gaze, puckered nipples, and pale skin splotched rose with desire kindled wild, unruly heat. His body ran wide open, and magic mingled with sex as he plumbed her. Sensation cascaded through him as she crested once, and then again. The third time, he abandoned control and juddered hard, matching her passion with his own.

Cradling her in his arms as their sexual heat faded from blazing hot to a simmer, he savored the moment. Tenderness mingled with the protectiveness that has swamped him earlier.

"Aye, lassie," he murmured in Gaelic. "We do, indeed, belong to each other."

You've reached the end of *Time's Curse*, second of the Elemental Witch books. I do hope you've enjoyed it. Please leave a review while the book is fresh in your mind. Doesn't have to be fancy. A line or two will do it.

Look for *Time's Hostage*, next in this series, early in 2019.

Meanwhile, if you enjoy witchy books, you might like my Demon Assassin series. A sample from *Witch's Bounty*, first of that series, follows.

Ann Gimpel is a USA Today bestselling author. A lifelong aficionado of the unusual, she began writing speculative fiction a few years ago. Since then her short fiction has appeared in many webzines and anthologies. Her longer books run the gamut from urban fantasy to paranormal romance. Once upon a time, she nurtured clients. Now she nurtures dark, gritty fantasy stories that push hard against reality. When she's not writing, she's in the backcountry getting down and dirty with her camera. She's published over sixty-five books to date, with several more planned for 2018 and beyond. A husband, grown children, grandchildren, and wolf hybrids round out her family.

Keep up with her at www.anngimpel.com or http://anngimpel.blogspot.com

If you enjoyed what you read, get in line for special offers and pre-release special reads. Newsletter Signup!

BOOK DESCRIPTION: WITCH'S BOUNTY

One of three remaining demon assassin witches, Colleen is almost the last of her kind. Along with her familiar, a changeling spirit, she was hoping for a few months of quiet, running a small magicians' supply store in Fairbanks, Alaska. Peace isn't in the cards, though. Demons are raising hell in Seattle. She's on her way to kick some serious demon ass, when a Sidhe shows up and demands she accompany him to England to quell a demon uprising.

The Sidhe might be the best-looking man Colleen's ever stumbled over, but she doesn't have time for him— or much of anything else. She, Jenna, and Roz are Earth's only hedge against being overrun by Hell's minions. Even with help from a powerful magic wielder like the Sidhe, the odds aren't good and the demons know it.

Sensing victory is within their grasp, they close in for the kill.

...In the beginning, Ceridwen bent over her cauldron, stirring up the world. Sometimes the other Celts helped, but mostly they left her alone because she was so ill tempered. She created witches somewhere between Sidhe, dark fae, and Druids—borrowing a pinch of this, and a bit of that, to give them an eclectic mix of magic.

Gwydion dropped by one day and leaned over her shoulder, peering into the large, black pot. "You've made the witches far too powerful," he complained.

Ceridwen shrugged. She pulled her staff out of the sludge simmering before her, dark eyes flashing dangerously. "Do you want this job?"

The master enchanter shook his head. Blond hair wafted in steam from the cauldron. "No, but you'll rue the day you didn't temper their magic."

The goddess narrowed her eyes. "Does Bran, god of prophecy, know you've taken over his job?"

Gwydion bristled. "Damn my eyes, woman, you've made witches as strong as the Sidhe."

She got to her feet, faced the other god, and thumped his chest with her long-nailed forefinger. "One day we may need that strength."

Gwydion looked as if he wanted to say something. Instead, his broad-shouldered form shimmered and disappeared.

"Humph. Good riddance." Ceridwen sank into a cross-legged sit next to her cauldron and went back to stirring. She'd die before admitting this to the other Celtic gods, but out of all her creations, witches were her favorite...

Rain worsened from a steady drizzle to a pounding, punishing deluge of icy sleet. Colleen Kelly strengthened the spell around herself. It sizzled where it ran up against the droplets. At least she wasn't quite as wet as she would have been without its protection. Pavement glistened wetly in the last of the day's light. It was just past three in the afternoon, but December days were short in the northern latitudes and Fairbanks was pretty far north.

"At least it's not snowing," she muttered as she pushed through a nearby glass-fronted door into the magicians' supply store she owned with two other witches in the older part of downtown. Bells hanging around the door pealed discordantly. She sent a small jolt of magic to silence them.

"I heard that. Not the bells, but you. It's supposed

to snow this time of year. How could you possibly be pleased the weather patterns have gone to hell?"

Jenna Neil stalked over to the coatrack where Colleen stood. Blonde hair, hacked off at shoulder level, framed a gamine's face and shrewd, hazel eyes. Jenna towered over Colleen's six foot height by a good four inches, and her broad shoulders would've made most men jealous. Between her trademark high-heeled boots and a scruffy embroidered red cloak tossed over skintight blue jeans, she looked as exotic as the anti-hex hoop earrings dangling from each ear.

Colleen rolled her eyes, shook out her coat, and hung it on the rack. "Spare me your lecture about global warming, okay? It's cold enough to snow. It just isn't, for some reason."

"Mmph." The line of Jenna's jaw tensed.

Indian spices wafted through the air, mingling with the scents of herbs, dried flowers, and desiccated body parts from small animals. Colleen's stomach growled. Breakfast had been at six that morning—a long time ago. Pretty bad when even dried newt smelled like food.

"Did you cook something?" she asked. "And if you did, is there any left?"

A terse nod. Jenna turned away, walking fast. Colleen lengthened her normal stride to catch up.

"Hey, sweetie. What happened? You can't be in this big a snit over the weather."

Jenna kept walking, heading for the small kitchen at the back of the store. "A lot of things. I was just having a cup of tea. Shop's been dead today." She disappeared behind a curtain.

Colleen glanced over one shoulder at the empty store. The phalanx of bells around the door would alert them if anyone stopped in. The minute she tugged the heavy, upholstery fabric that served as a kitchen door aside, the pungent tang of Irish whiskey made her eyes water. "You said tea."

"Yeah, well I spiked it."

Colleen grunted. "Smells like you took a bath in booze. What the fuck happened?" She grabbed the larger woman and spun her so they faced one another.

"We got another pay-your-tithe-or-die e-mail from our Coven." Jenna's nostrils flared in annoyance.

"So? That's like the tenth one." There were new policies none of them agreed with, so they'd joined with about twenty other witches and stopped paying the monthly stipend that supported their Coven's hierarchy.

"It's not what's bothering me." Jenna pulled free from Colleen, tipped her cup, and took a slug of what smelled like mostly liquor.

Colleen fought a desire to swat her. Getting to the

point quickly had never been one of Jenna's talents. She clamped her jaws together. "What is?"

"Roz called with...problems." Jenna turned and started toward the steep staircase ladder leading to her bedroom above the shop.

"You can't just drop that bomb and leave." Colleen made another grab for Jenna to keep her in the kitchen. Worry for their friend ate at her. Of the three of them, Roz was by far the most volatile. "What happened? I thought she was in Missouri, or maybe it was Oklahoma, visiting that dishy dude she met online."

"Didn't work out." The corners of Jenna's mouth twisted downward.

Colleen quirked a brow, urging her friend to say more.

Jenna plowed on. "He only wanted her for her magic. Turned out he preferred men."

"Aw, shit." Colleen blew out a breath. "She must've been disappointed."

Half a snorting laugh bubbled past Jenna's lips. "Maybe now she is. At the time, furious would've been closer to the mark."

Colleen's throat tightened. "Crap! What'd she do? She didn't hurt him, did she?"

"Not directly. She turned him over to the local Coven."

"Thank God!" Colleen let go of Jenna and laid a

hand over her heart. Roxanne Lantry was more than capable of killing anyone who pissed her off. It was how she ended up in Alaska. Roz hadn't exactly been caught when her cheating husband and his two girlfriends went missing, but she hadn't stuck around to encourage the authorities to question her, either.

Colleen and Jenna had already left Seattle when that little incident went down. Roz repressed her antipathy for Alaska's legendary foul weather and joined them. Magically, she was strong as an ox, and she had a hell of a temper.

Colleen's stomach growled again. Louder this time. It didn't give a good goddamn about anything other than its empty state. She pushed past Jenna to the stove, lifted a lid, and peered into a battered aluminum pot. Curry blasted her. The spicy odor stung her eyes and made her nose run.

"Whew. Potent. Mind if I help myself?"

"Go ahead." Jenna sat heavily in one of two chairs with a rickety wooden table between them. She picked up her mug and took another long swallow.

Dish in hand, Colleen slapped it on the table in front of the other chair and went in search of a mug of her own. There weren't any clean ones, so she plucked one out of the sink and rinsed it. Back at the stove, she tipped the teakettle. Thick, amber liquid spilled from its stubby snout into her waiting mug. Jenna waggled the whiskey bottle in her direction.

"Nah." Colleen settled at the table. "It would go right to my head. Maybe after I get some food on board." She tucked in. After the first few mouthfuls, when the curry powder nearly annihilated her taste buds, the pea, potato, and ham mixture wasn't half-bad.

Jenna drank steadily, not offering anything by way of conversation.

When Colleen's dish was empty, she refilled her mug with tea, filched a couple of biscuits from the cupboard, and sat back down. "Are you going to talk to me?"

"I suppose so." Jenna's words slurred slightly.

Colleen cocked her head to one side. "I suggest you start now, before you forget how."

"Oh, please." Jenna blew out a breath, showering the small space with whiskey fumes. Colleen waited. The other witch could be stubborn. Wheedling, cajoling, or urging wouldn't work until she was good and ready to talk.

Finally, after so long Colleen had nearly chewed a hole in her cheek, Jenna finally muttered, "Roz called."

Colleen ground her teeth together. "You already said that. It's how you knew what happened with the guy."

Jenna nodded. "There's more." She picked up the

whiskey, started to pour it into her mug, then apparently changed her mind and drank right from the bottle. "She's in Seattle. Checked in with Witches' Northwest, just to say hello, and because she wanted to touch base with people she's known for a long time."

Another long pause. Colleen batted back a compulsion spell. It wasn't nice to use those on your friends. She shoved her hands under her bottom to reduce the temptation.

Jenna lowered her voice until Colleen had to strain to hear. "The Irichna demons are back."

"But our last confrontation wasn't all that long ago. Only a few months. Sometimes when we best them, they've stayed gone for years."

Colleen shook her head. Even the sound of the word, *Irichna*, crackled against her ears, making them tingle unpleasantly. Irichna demons were the worst. Hands down, no contest. They worked for Abbadon, Demon of the Abyss. Evil didn't get much worse than that. No wonder Jenna was drinking. Colleen held her hand out for the bottle—suddenly a drink seemed like a most excellent idea—and picked her words with care. "Did Roz actually sight one?"

"Yeah. She also asked if we could come and help. More than asked. She came as close to begging as I've ever heard her."

"Erk. They have a whole Coven there. Several if

you count all the ones in western Washington. Why do they need us?" Colleen belted back a stiff mouthful of whiskey. It burned a track all the way to her stomach where it did battle with all the curry she'd eaten.

Jenna just shot her a look. "You know why."

Colleen swallowed again, hoping for oblivion, except it couldn't come quick enough. She knew exactly why, but the answer stuck in her craw and threatened to choke her. The three of them were the last of a long line of demon assassins, witches with specialized powers, able to lure demons, immobilize them, and send them packing to the netherworld.

When things worked right.

They often didn't, though, which was what killed off the other demon assassin witches. It didn't help that demons as a group had been gathering power these last fifty years or so. Witches lived for a long time, but they were far from immortal, and demon assassin ability was genetic. She, Jenna, or Roz would have to produce children or that strain of magic would die out. So far, none of them had come anywhere close to identifying a guy who looked like husband material...

Colleen looked at her hands. Even absent a husband, none of them had a shred of domesticity. Certainly not enough to saddle themselves with offspring.

"What's the matter?" Jenna grinned wickedly,

clearly more than a little drunk. "Cat got your tongue too?"

As if on cue, a blood-curdling meow rose from a shadowed corner of the kitchen and Bubba, Colleen's resident familiar, padded forward. When he was halfway to them, he gathered his haunches beneath him and sprang to the table. It rocked alarmingly, and Jenna made a grab for her cup. The large black cat skinned his lips back from his upper teeth, bared his incisors, and hissed.

"Oh, all right." Colleen clamped her jaws tight and summoned the magic to shift Bubba to his primary form, a gnarled three-foot changeling.

The air shimmered around him. Before it cleared, he swiped the liquor out of her hand and drained the bottle.

"Would've been a good reason to leave you a cat," Jenna mumbled.

He stood on the table and glared at both of them, elbows akimbo, bottle still dangling from his oversized fingers. "If you're going to fight demons, you have to take me with you."

"No, we don't," Colleen countered.

"You don't follow directions well," Jenna said pointedly.

"Isn't that the truth?" Colleen rotated her head from side to side, starting to feel the whiskey. At least once when they'd humored the changeling, he'd almost gotten all of them killed. Problem was she couldn't predict when he'd follow her orders, and when he'd decide on a different tack altogether. Then there were the times his fearlessness had saved them all.

Bubba might be a wildcard, but he was *her* wildcard.

"You forgot when I welcomed your spirit into my body—and kept it alive—while the healers worked on you." Bubba eyed Colleen, sounding smug.

"If you hadn't decided to play hero, and needed to be rescued, the demons wouldn't have injured me." Colleen winced at the sour undertone in her voice. That incident had happened five years before. Maybe it was time she got over it.

"Nevertheless." He tossed his shaggy head, thick with hair as black as the cat's. "When you conjured me from the barrows of Ireland, and bound me, we became a unit. You can't go off and leave me here. It would be like leaving a part of yourself behind." His dark eyes glittered with challenge.

"I hate to admit it—" Jenna sounded a little less drunk "—but he's right."

"See." Bubba leered at them, jumped off the table, and waddled over to the stove with his bowlegged gait. Once there, he opened the oven, climbed onto its door, and peeked into the pot. He started to stick a hand inside.

"Hold it right there, bud." Colleen got to her feet, covered the distance to the stove, and dished him up some of the curry mixture. "Get some clothes on and you can have this."

He clambered down from his perch and over to several colorful canisters scattered around the house where she stashed outfits for him. Keeping Bubba clothed had been a huge problem until she'd hatched up a plan and sewn him several pant and shirt combos with Velcro closures, since he didn't like buttons or zippers.

The changeling dressed quickly and took the bowl from her. "I could've gotten my own food."

"Better for the rest of us if you keep your paws out of the cook pot." Jenna stood a bit unsteadily. "I'll be right back."

Bubba stuffed food into his mouth with his fingers. "Where's she going?" His words came out garbled as he chewed open-mouthed.

Colleen looked away. "Probably to pee. Maybe to throw up. Um, look, Bubba, it might be wiser if we took a quick side trip to Ireland and released you."

She glanced sidelong at the changeling spirit she'd summoned during a major demon war forty years before. He'd been truly helpful then, especially after he'd mastered English, which hadn't taken him all that long. In the intervening time, he'd mostly clung to his feline form, eating and keeping their shop free of mice and rats. They'd lived in Seattle the first ten years or so after he joined them, relocating to Alaska to conceal their longevity. She dragged the heels of her hands down her face, feeling tired. It was getting close to time to move again, but she didn't want to think about it.

Bubba shook his head emphatically. Food flew from the sides of his mouth. He scooped a glob off the floor and ate it anyway. "I have to agree to being released. I don't want to go back to my barrow. I like it much better here."

Colleen sucked in a hollow breath, blew it out, and did it again. Bubba was right. Rules were rules. He'd had a choice at the front end. He could've refused her. Witches respected all living creatures. The ones on the good side of the road, anyway. No forced servitude for their familiars, despite rumors to the contrary.

Jenna lurched back into the kitchen looking a little green. "You okay?" Colleen asked.

"Yeah. I drank too much, that's all." She rinsed her mug at the sink, refilled it with tap water, and sat back down. "Did you two come up with a plan?"

"I'm going." Bubba left his dish on the floor and vaulted back onto the table.

Jenna rolled red-rimmed eyes. "That was the discussion when I left."

"Your point?" Colleen swallowed irritation.

"Nothing." The other witch sounded sullen, but maybe she just didn't feel well.

"I offered to free him—" Colleen began.

"I refused," Bubba cut in. He shook his head. "No recognition for all my years of loyal service. Tsk. You should be—"

"Stuff it." Jenna glared at him. "We have bigger problems than your wounded ego."

He stuck out his lower lip, looking injured as only a changeling spirit could, but he didn't say anything else.

"I suppose we have to go to Seattle," Colleen muttered, half to herself.

"Don't see any way around it." Jenna worried her lower lip between her teeth.

"What exactly did Roz say?"

"We didn't talk long. Her cellphone battery was almost dead." A muscle twitched beneath Jenna's eye. "She'd just stopped in at Coven Headquarters and the group mobbed her. Said we had to come. They've already lost about twenty witches to stealth demon attacks."

Colleen's heart skipped a few beats. Twenty witches was a lot. Maybe a quarter of the Witches' Northwest Coven. "Crap. When did the attacks start?"

"Only a few days ago. They'd planned to call us, but saw it as goddess intervention when Roz showed up."

"Damn that Oklahoma cowboy." Colleen pounded a fist into her open palm. "If his Coven doesn't flatten him, I will."

"He wasn't a cowboy." Jenna's voice held a flat, dead sound. "He was supposed to be a witch. You know, like us."

"Doesn't matter."

"Do you want to close things up here, or should I try to get someone from our Coven to fill in at the shop?" Jenna looked pale, but the tipsy aspect had left her face.

Colleen shook her head. "We haven't sold enough in the last few weeks to make it worthwhile to pay someone to clerk for us."

"Okay." Jenna's hazel eyes clouded with worry. "When do you want to leave?"

"If you asked Witches' Northwest, we probably should've left three days ago."

"How are we getting there?" Bubba squared his hunched shoulders as much as he could and eyed Colleen.

"Excellent question." Jenna looked at Colleen too.

She raised her hands in front of her face, palms out. "Stop it, you two. I can't deal with the pressure."

Colleen clamped her jaws together and considered their options. Roz already had a car in Seattle. It didn't make sense to drive their other one down, plus it would take too long. Flying with Bubba was impossible. He looked too odd in his gnome form and his cat form didn't do well with the pressure changes. They had to teleport, which would seriously deplete their magic and mean they couldn't fight so much as a disembodied spirit for at least twenty-four hours after they arrived.

Jenna screwed her face into an apologetic scowl, apparently having come to the same conclusion. "Look, I'm sorry I'm not more help. There's something about that particular mix of earth, fire, and air that I always bungle."

Air whistled through Colleen's teeth. It had been so long since they'd teleported anywhere, she'd almost forgotten Jenna's ineptitude with the requisite spell. "How about this? You go down to the basement and practice. I'll get a few things together..."

"What do you want me to do?" Bubba asked.

"You can help me," Jenna said. "I'll do better if I have an object to practice with."

The changeling scrunched his low forehead into a mass of wrinkles. "Just don't get me lost."

"Even if she does, I'll be able to find you." Colleen tried to sound reassuring. She was fond of her familiar. In many ways, he was very childlike.

Heh! Maybe that's why I've been so reluctant to have a kid. I already have one who'll never grow up.

The bells around the shop door clanged a discordant riot of notes. "Crap!" Jenna shot to her feet. "First customer in two days. I should've locked the damn door."

"Back to cat form." Colleen flicked her fingers at Bubba, who shrank obligingly and slithered out of clothing, which puddled around him. She snatched up his shirt and pants and dropped them back into the canister.

"I say," a strongly accented male voice called out. "Is anyone here?"

"I'll take care of the Brit," Colleen mouthed. "Take Bubba to the basement and practice."

She got to her feet and stepped past the curtain. "Yes?" She gazed around the dimly lit store for their customer.

A tall, powerfully built man, wearing dark slacks and a dark turtleneck, strode toward her, a woolen greatcoat slung over one arm. His white-blond hair was drawn back into a queue. Arresting facial bones—sculpted cheeks, strong jaw, high forehead—captured her attention and stole her breath. He was quite possibly the most gorgeous man she'd ever laid eyes on. Discerning green eyes zeroed in on her face, caught her gaze, and held it. Magic danced around him in a numinous shroud. Strong magic.

What was he?

And then she knew. Daoine Sidhe. The man had to be Sidhe royalty. No wonder he was so stunning it almost hurt to look at him.

Colleen held her ground. She placed her feet shoulder width apart and crossed her arms over her chest. "What can I help you with?"

"Colleen Kelly?"

Okay, so he knows who I am. Doesn't mean a thing. He's Sidhe. Could've plucked my name right out of my head.

"That would be me. How can I help you?" she repeated, burying a desire to lick nervously at her lips.

"Time is short. I've been hunting you for a while now. Come closer, witch. We need to talk."

Witch's Bane

Witches Rule

Dragon Lore

Highland Secrets

To Love a Highland Dragon

Dragon Maid

Dragon's Dare

Earth Reclaimed

Earth's Requiem

Earth's Blood

Earth's Hope

Elemental Witch

Timespell

Time's Curse

GenTech Rebellion

Winning Glory

Honor Bound

Claiming Charity

Loving Hope

Keeping Faith

Rubicon International

Garen

Lars

Soul Dance

Tarnished Beginnings

Tarnished Legacy

Tarnished Prophecy

Tarnished Journey

Soul Storm

Dark Prophecy

Dark Pursuit

Dark Promise

Underground Heat

Roman's Gold

Wolf Born

Blood Bond

Wolf Clan Shifters

Alice's Alphas

Megan's Mates

Sophie's Shifters

Wylde Magick

Gemstone

Lion's Lair

Unbalanced

~

STANDALONE BOOKS

Branded, That Old Black Magic Romance (paranormal romance)

Edge of Night (short story collection, paranormal and horror)

Grit is a 4-Letter Word (nonfiction)

Heart's Flame (post-apocalyptic romance)

Icy Passage (science fiction romance)

Marked by Fortune (post-apocalyptic coming of age story)

Melis's Gambit (historical paranormal romance)

Midnight Magic (paranormal romance)

Red Dawn (post-apocalyptic paranormal romance)

Shadow Play (historical paranormal romance)

Shadows in Time (Highland time travel romance)

Since We Fell (contemporary romance)

Warin's War (paranormal romance)